Praise for *Guiding Instruction in Young Adult Literature*

"The authors believe that students reading young adult literature are in a transformational period of their lives. The young adult literature that they encounter and engage in can be companions and guides as they explore and develop their identities and develop their capacity for tolerance, understanding, compassion, equity, and kindness. The authors provide not only a framework rooted in Rosenblatt's concept of transactional reading, but they also provide models for applying the instructional framework to actual young adult stories. Their coverage of the theory and practice of the young adult literature landscape puts teachers in a position to develop their own young adult literature lessons, units, and curriculum knowing they are building on the ground that will encourage student engagement and involvement with the power of young adult literature."

—**Michael Deasy**, EdD, reading teacher

"This book is an eye-opening resource for anyone working with young adults in the English language arts, as well as anyone simply interested in young adult literature. Both practitioners and researchers will find this book an informative resource on the literary and psychological theories informing the instruction of young adult literature, and educators especially will find helpful the suggestions for instruction offered by the authors. This is a must-read for anyone working with young people in the field of literature."

—**Andrea Mooney**, PhD, English teacher, Reading Memorial High School

"The prose is pithy, and for one, it aptly orients the reader toward the theme of identity. The authors crafted a work that promotes higher-order thinking in literacy classrooms. Their foundational model emphasizes identity, empathy, compassion, and understanding over quick recall, standardization, and other less desirable things. Amazing work! Now all they need to do is find enlightened and open-minded teachers willing to leave their old ways behind."

—**Matthew Sutton**, PhD, disabled veteran outreach program specialist, Greater New Bedford Career Center

"The authors' choice to begin the book with so much attention to identity formation in young adult literature is a good one. Historically, concerns about adolescent identity have been besieged by so many warring factions. There often are many unhealthy distractions and messages mixed in with well-meaning advice leaving teachers and students feeling a bit confused. Therefore, this book is valuable as it provides clear reasoning and guidance for English teachers to help students, through literature, to reconcile such conflicting perspectives at such a challenging point in their lives."

—**Raymond Pape**, EdD, English teacher,
Hamilton-Wenham Regional High School, and
adjunct English professor, Endicott College

"Two of the writing purposes of this book match the mainstream of educational requirements and a nationwide movement initiated by the Chinese government to strengthen and improve ideological instruction and moral education in all levels of the educational system, especially colleges and universities where disciplinary instruction is expected to integrate ideological and moral education for students in various ways. These writing purposes are acquainting readers with the dimensions of the human experience that young adult literature offers because of its reinforcement of such values as tolerance, acceptance, understanding, compassion, empathy, and kindness, and reminding readers that society is in desperate need of thoughtful citizens and that young adult literature provides rich resources for students to draw on in order to grow into compassionate, engaged, and educated citizens and the needs of society."

—**Wei Xu**, EdD, associate professor,
Shanghai International Studies University

"This is a valuable and informative book. In today's dramatically changing world, it is extremely important for all of us to think about how we educate the young adults who are the key to the future. One of the most effective ways to help them deal with uncertainty and to keep them sharp and reflective is through their reading. This book provides detailed discussions and instructive insights not only for current and future teachers but also for parents and other educators who hope to have a better understanding of adolescents and to use the power of young adult literature to help young people navigate through their journey of life. Readers will find a variety of practical suggestions to support young adults such as evaluating and selecting the right books, using effective questioning strategies, and guiding readers to relish the stories and to explore bigger themes."

—**Qing Zhao**, EdD, curriculum coordinator,
Boston CINE (Chinese in New England)

Guiding Instruction in Young Adult Literature

Guiding Instruction in Young Adult Literature

Ideas from Theory, Research, and Practice

Lorraine Dagostino, Jennifer Bauer, and Kathleen Ryan

ROWMAN & LITTLEFIELD
Lanham • Boulder • New York • London

Published by Rowman & Littlefield
An imprint of The Rowman & Littlefield Publishing Group, Inc.
4501 Forbes Boulevard, Suite 200, Lanham, Maryland 20706
www.rowman.com

6 Tinworth Street, London SE11 5AL, United Kingdom

Copyright © 2021 by Lorraine Dagostino, Jennifer Bauer, Kathleen Ryan

All rights reserved. No part of this book may be reproduced in any form or by any electronic or mechanical means, including information storage and retrieval systems, without written permission from the publisher, except by a reviewer who may quote passages in a review.

British Library Cataloguing in Publication Information Available

Library of Congress Cataloging-in-Publication Data

Names: Dagostino, Lorraine, 1947- author. | Bauer, Jennifer, 1975- author. | Ryan, Kathleen (Professor), author.
Title: Guiding instruction in young adult literature : ideas from theory, research and practice / Lorraine Dagostino, Jennifer Bauer and Kathleen Ryan.
Description: Lanham : Rowman & Littlefield, [2021] | Includes bibliographical references. | Summary: "This book provides a careful and compassionate analysis of the relationship between a young adult reader and a literary text from both psychological and sociological perspectives"—Provided by publisher.
Identifiers: LCCN 2021009194 (print) | LCCN 2021009195 (ebook) | ISBN 9781475853254 (cloth) | ISBN 9781475853261 (paperback) | ISBN 9781475853278 (epub)
Subjects: LCSH: Young adult literature—Study and teaching—United States. | Young adult literature—Psychological aspects. | Youth—Books and reading—United States.
Classification: LCC PN1008.8 .D35 2021 (print) | LCC PN1008.8 (ebook) | DDC 809/.892830712—dc23
LC record available at https://lccn.loc.gov/2021009194
LC ebook record available at https://lccn.loc.gov/2021009195

*To all of the young adults that we have taught, and
to others who have worked with them.
We thank them for their insights.
To future young adults and those who will know them, we wish
them a good journey through the worlds that they cannot know
except through the literature that they choose to read.*

Contents

Preface — xi

Acknowledgments — xiii

Introduction — 1

1 A Conceptual Understanding of Literature and Young Adult Literature — 3

2 Theoretical Perspectives on the Literary, Psychological, and Sociological Aspects of Young Adults' Identity and Growth — 33

3 The Role that Questions and Inquiry Play in Nurturing an Understanding of Young Adult Literature — 67

4 Media, Technology, and Literature — 83

5 The Conceptual Background and Practical Ideas for the Instructional Goals for the Development of Identity in Young Adult Literature — 99

6 Final Remarks and Implications for the Implementation of Curriculum Organization and Content — 123

Background Reading and Bibliographic References — 141

About the Authors — 149

Preface

Guiding Instruction in Young Adult Literature: The Ideas from Theory, Research and Practice

Lorraine Dagostino, Kathleen Ryan, and Jennifer Bauer

OVERVIEW OF THE CONTENT AND THE ORGANIZATION OF THE BOOK

Our purpose for writing this book, *Guiding Instruction in Young Adult Literature: The Ideas from Theory, Research and Practice*, is to share with practicing educators a conceptual framework and specific ideas for instruction for use with young adult literature. The focus of the instruction is for readers who are eleven to twenty-one years old of various abilities.

The approach varies from many standard approaches to such instruction by focusing on higher-order thinking with the goal of helping readers have an interesting and a meaningful experience with the literature that they read—both classic and contemporary selections. The approach encourages participation and interaction among the students and with the teacher.

The guidance for instruction is simplified, and the process for developing instructional plans is illustrated. The theme of identity through growth, both for encouraging the personal development of the young adult reader and as a conceptual topic in literature, is the organizing structure for the content of the work.

From our experience in the classroom, we have found that this type of instruction is engaging for young adult readers, and that it is helpful to teachers seeking ways to appeal to the avid reader and the reluctant reader. The nature of this instruction requires an immersion in the reading that develops a good understanding of the themes and the issues prevalent in young adult literature such that it enhances the personal development and the growth of the young person. We believe that this is an important goal for reading at this age, and that it needs to be accomplished in an interesting and meaningful way.

The material in this book is rooted in a philosophy of instruction of literature that has its underpinnings in Louise Rosenblatt's concept of transactional reading. This view encourages the reader to bring his or her own experiences to the text to shape the interpretation of the text while preserving the integrity of the text and the author's meaning. The content for instruction represents a developmental view of the transformative growth of the young adult reader derived from psychological and sociological perspectives and theory.

The book is organized to describe these underpinnings, and then to show how they can be translated into everyday practices. This means that there is a discussion of the conceptual framework of this type of instruction that is followed by various instructional activities. We believe that this type of instruction will engage the young adult reader as well as teach important aspects of literature in a manner useful to the young adult reader.

The suggestions for instruction range from complete lessons to mini-lessons with discussion on how to integrate these suggestions into each day's reading. The suggestions for instruction also describe activities and approaches that are initiated, developed, and implemented by the young adult reader in ways that encourage them to take responsibility for their learning. There is a section on integrating media, technology, and literature into instruction too. Finally, the ideas in the book help the teacher with the process of guiding curriculum and the development of related instruction.

A comparison with other books on the market shows that this book is distinctive from these books with regards to instructional purposes, or for professional development. This book meets both of those objectives. Again, the focus of this work is instruction, supported by literary, psychological, and sociological theory, for the reader in the age range of eleven to twenty-one years old and of various abilities.

Acknowledgments

Writing a book always needs the support of others. For this support, we thank families and friends who gave us the time to do the work, including Kendra Bauer. We thank the students who have let us guide them on their journey through reading young adult literature. We thank our editors, Tom Koerner and Carlie Wall, for their guidance in doing this work.

We also thank several people who read the manuscript and made kind remarks in the final days of the writing: Matthew Sutton, Andrea Mooney, Raymond Pape, Kendra Bauer, Christian LeBlanc, Qing Zhao, Michael Deasy, Joann Burket, Mary Robbins, Linda Erichson, Wei Xu. These people brought to their reading many years of work as educators, and in some instances parents of young adults. They also brought their experience as lifelong readers to the reading.

We now thank you for choosing to read what we believe that we have to offer you.

Introduction

The questions that most writers must answer are "Is this project worth doing?" and "What do we hope to accomplish by writing this particular book?" The three of us, after many conversations, decided it would be worth the time and work to share our thoughts and insights with others who work with young adults. We thought that the book would be helpful in several ways.

First, the book explores young adult literature, literary theories, models, and various approaches to teaching literature in the classroom. For those who have an interest in teaching older children, this book gives a glimpse into both the literature written for students between the ages of eleven and twenty-one and the literary, psychological, and sociological theories, models, and approaches that support the use of young adult literature in the classroom.

Second, this book can enhance our effectiveness when engaging with anyone interested in working with adolescents. We think that this is the case because the central theme of most young adult fiction is focused on the journey of becoming an adult and finding an answer to the question "Who am I and who do I want to become?." Young adult literature offers all of us the opportunity to better understand all young people, but especially those young people who feel invisible, overlooked, or neglected because of their sexual orientation, cultural backgrounds, physical limitations, or personal struggles.

Third, the book acquaints readers with the dimensions of the human experience that young adult literature offers. Young adult literature has the capacity to open hearts and minds to reinforce such values as tolerance, acceptance, understanding, compassion, empathy, and kindness.

Finally, the book reminds us that society is in desperate need of thoughtful citizens, and that young adult literature provides a deep well for students to draw from in order to grow into the compassionate, engaged, and educated citizens society needs. We need our students to experience literature and to work for the principles of equality and the principles of freedom within the context of the qualities of empathy, compassion, and concern for others.

Our hope is that our decision to focus the book on the idea of the theme of identity in young adulthood accomplishes these four goals.

Chapter 1

A Conceptual Understanding of Literature and Young Adult Literature

OVERVIEW OF CHAPTER 1

The key components of the conceptual and theoretical framework for this book include a conceptual understanding of literature and young adult literature, an understanding of the significant themes in novels and the ways themes can be related to the development of the young adult reader, an awareness of the historical origins of young adult literature, and a sense of the important place literature has in the virtual community.

These understandings give us the context for examining how Louise Rosenblatt's view on transactional reading contributes to a personal and intellectual reading of literature and young adult literature as well as to psychological and sociological perspectives on identity and transformative growth. These understandings show how young adult literature has been transformed over the years so that it has become more acceptable for instruction and for independent reading.

Finally, acknowledging that the nature of literacy has evolved and continues to evolve, we address how the virtual community influences and can be integrated into the reading of young adult literature.

QUESTIONS GUIDING THE READING

What is literature and why read it?
How is young adult literature different from literature in general and why is it important?
What kind of reading contributes to the young adult reader's development?
What is the history and the evolution of young adult literature?

What are the causes of the changes in young adult literature?
What is the place of young adult literature in the school curriculum?
Can the virtual community be integrated into the school curriculum?

LITERATURE

What are the primary characteristics of literature: substance, form, and influencing factors?

Defining Literature

Defining literature requires a focus on the substance of universal themes and language, primary characteristics, and distinguishing marks and form as evidenced in genre and text structure. The influencing factors such as audiences, readers' expectations, and general issues and goals are important.

Substance: Universal Themes and Language

Developing a definition of literature requires addressing the formal and the informal aspects of the discussions and the definitions found in the writing about the concept of literature. To do so, we focus on the substance of the universal themes and the language that constitute literature as a form of writing in any culture. Having this focus helps us to see how literature helps readers to see the world with a wider lens than one's own experiences and personal world.

This focus also helps us to see how language can shape one's thinking and a view of the world, while conveying the values of any society through the personal or intellectual framework implicit in the message. The reader learns of the social environment and conditions the author portrays in the text along with the development of the characters who carry the essence of the message through their lives and actions.

Literature carries the universal themes of a society that express the ideas influencing humanity and depicting social circumstances and human dilemmas. Understanding the essence of the messages of literature through universal themes enhances our understanding of life and the human experience. Literature depicts these universal themes through both a good story and exposition.

Literature contributes to our understandings of life experiences in many ways. In most cases, literature encourages reflection on life's situations through various forms of language, and it extends the reader's reach into the world that they cannot experience, or know directly.

Through literature, language carries those universal themes, emotions, and thoughts. Literature has been the experimental playground for innovation in language in the expression of the themes of human experiences. The author's literary playground rests on the use of the primary characteristics of language as presented in the next section.

The Primary Characteristics of Literature

Beyond what we hope that reading literature achieves, it has been conceptualized by identifying specific primary characteristics and distinguishing marks such as how the metaphors shaping the writing carry those universal themes through language. These characteristics are the vehicles for structuring the text, either fictional or nonfictional, and giving us the many genres and text structures used in writing. Without them, we simply may have words with little substance and universal staying power.

To assist our understanding of this idea, we identify primary characteristics of literature with brief descriptions of each characteristic. The following figures 1.1 and 1.2 and the accompanying text attempt to meet this goal.

In addition to these literary elements, poetic language adds vividness to the meaning in all kinds of literature and takes the following forms.

The understanding of universal themes and language is enhanced with an understanding of form through knowledge of genre and structure.

Form: Genre and Structure

Like universal themes and language, we see a contribution to meaning in literature through the form of a text. Here is where we consider genre and text structure as part of the writing and the literary experience.

We believe that different genres reflect the multiplicity of ways that literature is shaped by the variation in story structure or exposition that may have an effect on the reader. We believe that different genres can convey similar messages differently. This may extend the appeal of the message to different readers, with some of the reasons being related to the differing ways that individual readers may process texts and language in general.

Because of this perspective, we encourage the reading of different genres early on in a reader's experiences with literature to develop openness on

Literary Element	Definition
Plot	the sequence of events or actions in a short, story, novel, play or narrative poem
Characterization	the means by which an author reveals a character's personality; an author can achieve multi-dimensional characters by describing a character's physical appearance, recording conversations, revealing a character's thoughts, revealing the perceptions of other characters, and showing the actions of the character
Setting	the time and place in which events in a short, story, novel, play, or narrative poem occur; a setting may simply serve as a physical background, but a writer may use the setting to establish a particular atmosphere in a work
Theme	the underlying idea that unites the plot, characters, and setting; the theme of a story and the moral of the story are not the same; the moral is a lesson, a rule to live by; a theme is a comment or belief about life; this belief or idea transcends cultural barriers and is usually universal in nature
Style	the writer's characteristic way of writing, determined by the choice of words, the arrangement of words in sentences, and the relationship of the sentences to one another
Point of View	In the *first-person* point of view, the story is told by one of the characters in his or her own words, and the reader is told only what this character knows and observes
	In the *third person* point of view, the narrator is not a character in the story at all; the third person narrator might tell a story from a *limited* point of view, focusing on only one character in the story; the third-person narrator, might, on the other hand, be an all-knowing or *omniscient*, observer who describes and comments on *all* characters and actions in the story

Figure 1.1. Literary Elements.

the part of the reader to the influence of genre on the author's meaning. We encourage a variation in the selection of genre for young adults to help the reader see larger worlds that are shaped in ways beyond the way that they usually see things. The sample illustrations of lessons presented in a later chapter will illustrate some of these ideas.

The hope is that readers can understand a piece of literature from the author's perspective. We hope that readers understand that authors choose a specific genre because it is appropriate for the "story or message" that the author wishes to convey and that authors often find a style and genre niche comfortable for their own use of language to say what they want to say.

We hope that the reader understands how the text structure is integral to and a product of the genre chosen to convey the message. The hope is that the story line or the text structure in literature is strong and cohesive so that it tells the stories of the differences in peoples' lives and how different values

Element	Definition	
Speaker	the voice created by a writer in a work	
Imagery	mental pictures created by language that appeals to the senses	
Diction	word choice	
Tone	the attitude of the speaker toward subject, self, and audience	
Irony	a contrast (between what is said and what is meant, or between things as they are and things as they appear to be)	
Figurative Language: imaginative, nonliteral language	*Simile*: nonliteral comparison of two people, places, feelings, things, using *like* or *as*	
	Metaphor: nonliteral comparison that omits *like* and *as*	
	Personification: attribution of human characteristics or emotions to inanimate objects	
	Synecdoche: use of a part to represent the whole	
	Metonymy: reference through a closely related object	
	Hyperbole: intentional overstatement (exaggeration)	
	Litotes: intentional understatement	
	Allusion: brief reference to well-known person, place or thing	
	Onomatopoeia: reflection of meaning in a word's sound	
	Synaesthesia: use of one sense to capture the experience of another sense	
Symbol	a concrete item that both represents itself and stands for more than itself	
Sound Devices: sound patterns that draw on repetition of sound and language units	*Rhyme*: repetition of a final word part, in *perfect rhyme* or in *slant (near rhyme)*	
	Alliteration: repetition of consonant sounds	
	Assonance: repetition of vowel sounds	
Rhythm: pattern of movement in language	*Meter*: pattern of stressed and unstressed syllables	
	Iambic foot: foot consisting of an unstressed and a stressed syllable	
	Trochaic foot: foot consisting of a stressed and an unstressed syllable	
	Anapest: foot consisting of two unstressed and one stressed syllable	
	Dactyl: foot consisting of one stressed and two unstressed syllables	
	Syllabic verse: verse characterized by a fixed syllable count in each line	
	Blank verse: verse characterized by unrhymed iambic pentameter	
Stanza: a poem's structural unit	*Quatrain*: four-line stanza	
	Couplet: pair of rhyming lines	
Form: arrangement of a poem with respect to meter and stanza	*Closed Form*: structure exhibiting regular metric, stanzaic, and/or rhyme patterning	
	Open Form: structure exhibiting organic shape rather than regular meter and rhyme	
	Free verse: poetry that does not exhibit consistent metrical regularity	
	Sonnet: fixed poetic form, fourteen lines in length and written in iambic pentameter	
	Ballad: poem written on a romantic subject, typically characterized by tragedy and understatement, and often arranged in ballad quatrains	
	Haiku: Japanese fixed form consisting of seventeen syllables arranged in three unrhymed lines of five, seven, and five syllables	
	Villanelle: nineteen-line fixed form, arranged in five tercets and a quatrain and following a specified rhyme and line repetition pattern	
Lineation: the division of verse into lines	*Enjambment*: line break in verse that does not correspond to a natural language pause	
	End-stop: line break that corresponds to a natural sentence of phrase break	
Theme	central message or idea	

Figure 1.2. Poetic Language.

influence those peoples' lives. We hope that the young adult reader can see how narrative, or exposition, can differ within a specific genre to tie together events as well as the tone and tension of each text to tell its tale.

This understanding of how genre and structure function together can advance the reader's understanding of a literary reading of a book. The reader's

Fiction	*Traditional Literature*: This is the genre, which contains folktales, myths, legends, and fairy tales. These stories, while each has distinguishing characteristics, share the element of having been passed down orally from generation to generation. Many of these stories can now be found in written form.	
	Fantasy: This genre usually contains elements that are not realistic such as talking animals or magical powers. Fantasy is often characterized by a departure from the way we ordinarily perceive the world around us. Fantasy includes science fiction as well as modern fantasy.	
	Realistic Fiction: Although stories in this genre are the product of the writer's imagination, these stories could actually happen. In this genre, the characters, setting, and dialogue are believable, the problems faced by the characters are realistically portrayed, and the resolution is credible.	
	Science Fiction: This genre is a type of fiction that is notable for dealing mainly with the impact of science, either real or imagined, on individuals with a society or on a society as a whole.	
	Historical Fiction: This genre is a type of fiction that, although it is a product of the author's imagination, has some elements that are true to the time period of the past in which it takes place.	
Non-Fiction	*Informational*: The primary purpose of this genre is to provide ideas and facts in order to inform the reader about the natural or social world. Informational text contains a variety of structures such as table of contents, labels, and glossaries to assist the reader in finding information efficiently and in better understanding the material.	
	Biography: A biography is a written account or a written history of a person's life written by someone other than the main person in the text.	
	Autobiography: An autobiography is an account of a person's life written by the person themself.	
	Memoir: A memoir falls under the genre of Autobiography. The main difference between a memoir and an autobiography is that a memoir is a more specific type of storytelling that often focuses on personal and specific memories, while an autobiography usually spans the entire life of the subject.	

Figure 1.3. Genres.

knowledge of genre and structure is crucial to giving an appropriate literary context to a text. Figure 1.3 should be helpful for you to recall genre types.

Being able to identify the genre of a book heightens the reader's ability to bring a broader literary context to the book. This context enhances the in-depth meaning of the text and the author's intentions for writing the book and conveying a particular meaning.

The Influencing Factors: Audience, Expectations, Goals, and Issues

Related, yet separate from substance and form, are other influencing factors shaping our concept of literature. These factors are the audience, the readers' expectations, and the goals and issues related to defining literature. With regards to audience, we can see that there can be a range of audiences for the focus of a piece, even when the author has a young adult reader in mind. This is an important idea because through literature we see life's experiences depicted for different audiences from various points of view with different purposes in mind. This may explain why and how different audiences read the same pieces differently.

With regards to readers' expectations to the text for good characterization as well as the language and other literary characteristics found in literary works, these expectations may be based upon formal knowledge or personal experiences. The key question is "How do readers' expectations and purposes influence the reading and the evaluation of a piece of literature, or simply influence the readers' general like or dislike for any given text?"

Guiding our thinking on some of the above ideas are the goals and issues related to instruction that helps the young adult reader appreciate various types of literature, hoping that the literature enlightens and gives pleasure to the reader. To do this we ask "Why read literature?" and "What purposes does it serve individual readers?" and "What do we hope will be the outcomes of reading literature as a part of contributing to specific outcomes of literacy?" Answers to these questions give us the goals and issues relative to instruction.

WHY READ LITERATURE? WHAT PURPOSES DOES IT SERVE?

General Thoughts

If a group of avid readers, teachers, or researchers were asked to answer the question "Why read literature?" the answers would vary. One person might respond that reading literature nurtures the imagination. Another might offer the response that reading literature helps improve writing skills. Others may say that reading literature is especially important today in an age when we communicate through texts, email, and social media because engaging with literature gives us the opportunity to sustain attention as we follow complicated texts and complex plotlines. Perhaps others might point out that literature has the power to open our hearts by helping us develop a sense of empathy and compassion, two traits that are oftentimes sorely lacking in our modern world. Perhaps an even more compelling reason is that literature can help develop the moral sensibility to deal with the complex ethical issues that we confront in an ever-changing world. These responses reflect the belief that reading literature can be transformative.

Although many excellent reasons to read and study literature exist, the facts lead us to the conclusion that although reading literature has many invaluable benefits, reading for pleasure has declined.

The Amount of Literature Read

The National Endowment for the Arts (NEA) began tracking reading and arts participation in 1982, when the literature reading rate was 54 percent. Since then, a decline in reading literature has been documented in the NEA surveys. In the NEA survey conducted in 2002, the percentage of Americans reading literature declined to 46.7 percent. According to the more recent survey of 2012, the percentage of American adults who read at least one type of literature, that is, any novels or short stories, reflected a slight drop to 45.2 percent.

In the most recent survey of the NEA of 2017, the percentage of Americans who read novels or short stories has fallen below historical levels to 41.8 percent. While this decline is concerning, it should be noted that the area of reading poetry and plays has increased in the U.S. adult population from 2012 (6.7%) to 2017(11.7%). This increase may reflect a renewed interest in literature and its transformative power.

The NEA's numbers are meant to capture reading for pleasure. They exclude required readings for work or school. The statistics related to the reading of young adults are similar. A study by Twinge and her colleagues (2019) who examined trends in media use in nationally representative samples of eighth, tenth, and twelfth graders in the United States from the years 1976 to 2016 showed, as most people would expect, digital media use has increased considerably. In 2016, the average twelfth grader was spending more than twice as much time online as in 2006, and the time online, texting, and on social media was totaling to about six hours a day by 2016. Whereas only half of twelfth graders visited social media sites almost every day in 2008, 82 percent did by 2016. This time online was accompanied by less time with print media.

Young adults in the 2010s spent significantly less time on print media compared with adolescents in previous decades. The percentage of twelfth grades that read a book or a magazine every day declined from 60 percent in the late 1970s to 16 percent by 2016. Although this decline is extremely concerning, we must acknowledge some positive studies. The 2006 Yankelovitch-Scholastic study reported that 51 percent of the five to seventeen year olds said they hadn't read books for pleasure until the Harry Potter series (Cart, 2007). Although many librarians and teachers attest to a renewed interest in reading, the challenge of educators is to acknowledge the decline, and then work to reverse it by building on any renewed interest in reading.

The reasons for this decline in reading are complicated, and contributing issues such as race, class, poverty, technology, and equity are exceedingly complex. Yet, oftentimes at the core of these complex issues is the individual's struggle to develop their identity within a culture that they perceive as foreign. Literature has the power to assist students as they develop their identities.

To ensure that all students experience the transformative power of literature, we must consider the role of schools and literacy instruction. Given the power of social media, there is increased pressure on schools to assist students in discovering the power of literature.

Literature instruction needs to have a dual focus: teachers must teach children the skills necessary to access the texts teachers present, and teachers must simultaneously present works of literature in a way that will engage students in thought, emotion, and dialogue. This type of engagement will lead students to experience literature and to discover many of those same emotions unfolding in literature in many ways.

A teacher's approach to literature matters, and the literary theories of Louise Rosenblatt provide a theoretical framework that embodies a teaching approach that has at its core a commitment to the transformative power of literature. Rosenblatt's views and the application and the implications of her views are presented in chapter 2 to give a more complete representation of hers and our work. Her views are then coupled with work from psychology and sociology to complete the theoretical framework for this book.

THE OUTCOMES OF LITERACY AS THEY RELATE TO LITERATURE

We extend the present discussion by looking at some additional specific outcomes of literacy that rest upon, or are part of, the outcomes of reading literature. These outcomes come from other works and are presented here in a conceptual model of outcomes of literacy developed by Dagostino and Carifio (1994).

As suggested earlier, empathy, compassion, and understanding are important outcomes related to reading literature because of how they extend our ability to get to a deeper meaning about life from what we read. We believe that careful readings of literature encourage a reflection on experiences to understand how people can lead different lives and illustrate their journeys through different circumstances.

The empathy, compassion, and the understanding derived from the reading of literature can help readers develop a values system that can guide the reader's life without judging others with different value systems. This outcome of literacy model has the development of empathy, compassion, and understanding as its fundamental goal in reading literature.

THE OUTCOMES OF LITERACY MODEL

We believe that there are specific outcomes of literacy related to reading literature as reflected in the abovementioned model. The conceptual Outcomes of Literacy Model based upon these outcomes takes these forms.

The model consists of two significant components: *The Context of Discourse* (see figures 1.4 & 1.5) and *The Understanding and Expression of Thought and Emotion* (see figure 1.6). The first major component, *The Context of Discourse*, concerns itself with three subcomponents of Situation, Vantage Points, and Content and Language. The second major component, *The Understanding and Expression of Thought and Emotion*, has two subcomponents—Awareness of Human Experiences and Responsible Communication of Individual and Collective Thought.

In both sets of subcomponents we see specific factors that make the subcomponent more concrete and definable. In the case of Situation we see three factors: Purpose, Audience, and Time and Place as the focal points of the concept of Situation. In the case of Vantage Points the three factors giving focus to the concept are Disciplinary Perspectives, Conceptual and Theoretical Orientation, and Point of View. In the case of Content and Language, we see four defining factors: Significance, Understanding and Judgment of Ideas, Nature of Themes, and Conversation and the Degree of Abstraction. In the

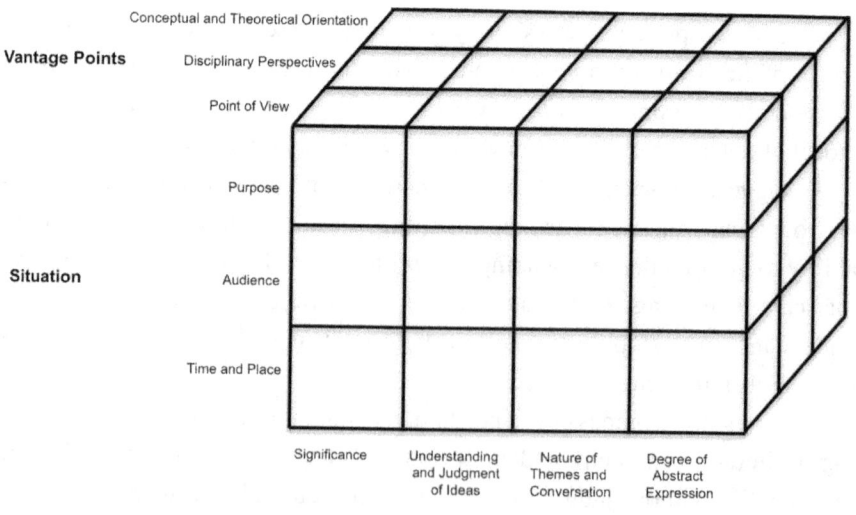

Figure 1.4. The Context of Discourse.

The Context of Discourse	The Understanding and Expression of Thought and Emotion
Situation Purpose Audience Time and Place *Vantage Points* Disciplinary Perspectives Conceptual and Theoretical Orientation Point of View *Content and Language* Significance Understanding and Judgment of Ideas Nature of Themes and Conversations Degree of Abstract Expression	*Awareness of Human Experiences and Dilemmas* Social Sensitivity Empathy Tolerance Openness *Responsible Communication of Individual and Collective Thought* **Schemas:** Shared Knowledge Informed Opinions and Decisions **Cognitive Activities:** Questioning Systematic Inquiry Specialized Schemas **Judicious Thought:** Selection of Appropriate Form of Communication Flexibility in Language and Thinking **Aesthetic Forms:** Creative Expression Eloquence of Language Metaphoric Thinking

Figure 1.5. The Outcomes of Literacy: The Context of Discourse and the Understanding and Expression of Thought and Emotion.

reading of literature, we see all of these factors merging and being integrated so that an in-depth reading can occur.

As we examine the subcomponents of *The Understanding and Expression of Thought and Emotion*, we see the subcomponent of Awareness of Human Expression defined by four factors: Social Sensitivity, Empathy, Tolerance, and Openness. In the case of Responsible Communication of Individual and

Awareness of Human Experiences and Dilemmas	Social Sensitivity
	Empathy
	Tolerance
	Openness

Responsible Communication of Individual and Collective Thought	Schemas	Shared Knowledge
		Informed Opinions and Decisions
	Cognitive Activities	Questioning
		Systematic Inquiry
		Specialized Schemes
	Judicious Thought	Selection of Appropriate Forms of Communication
		Flexibility in Language and Thinking
	Aesthetic Forms	Creative Expression
		Eloquence of Language
		Metaphoric Thinking

Figure 1.6. The Outcomes of Literacy: The Understanding and Expression of Thought and Emotion.

Collective Thought we see four factors with additional sub-factors. The four factors and sub-factors are as follows:

Schema: Shared Knowledge, Informed Opinion, Decisions
Cognitive Activity: Questioning, Systematic Inquiry, Specialized Schemas
Judicious Thought: Selection of Appropriate Forms of Communication, Flexibility in Language and Thought
Aesthetic Forms: Creative Expression, Eloquence of Language, Metaphoric Thinking

While the entire model is relevant to identifying the outcomes of literacy, some parts of the two components may weigh more heavily in relationship to reading literature. The visuals and summaries that draw together the subcomponents of each major component should be helpful in seeing how these outcomes are what constitute a good reading of literature. These components represent the product of a literate reading of a text.

The subcomponent of Awareness of Human Experiences and Dilemmas is at the heart of the emotional and the personal response we hope to help readers achieve when reading literature. The subcomponent of Responsible Communication of Individual and Collective Thought is at the heart of the intellectual responses that we hope readers achieve when they read at the next level to access the in-depth literary reading of a text.

From the model, we see that the first component, *The Context of Discourse*, gives us a framework for instructing the reader in reading any type of literature. Vantage Points asks the reader to find the "voice" of the writing and place it in a time and place. Situation focuses on finding the "voice" by contextualizing why and for whom the literature was written. Content and Language helps us determine its worth and how well the message is conveyed. It is a tool for guiding both an intellectual and a personal reading of a text. Developing an understanding of how these three factors influence text meaning is crucial to bringing literature to life.

The second component, *The Understanding and Expression of Thought and Emotion*, is a tool for determining our success in teaching young adults how to gain understanding of various aspects of meaning and responses as well as how to develop ways to convey messages. The first subcomponent, Awareness of Human Experiences and Dilemmas, is at the heart of why we teach literature and Rosenblatt's view on its value in our lives. The second subcomponent, Responsible Communication of Individual and Collective Thought, reminds us of the social relationships of literature, both personally and intellectually.

These two components of the model bring together much of how we need to approach a piece of literature and what we hope to gain from reading literature. Without a synthesis of each of these components and subparts, students do not gain a full personal or intellectual understanding from literature. With this theoretical framework in mind, we return to our general concerns about reading literature.

With some sense of the importance of reading literature in general established, it is time to ask "Do people read literature?," "Why young adult literature?," and "In What ways can young adult literature enhance a young adult's experience and ability to read literature?"

DO PEOPLE READ LITERATURE? IF SO, HOW MUCH? IF NOT, WHY NOT?

In considering the question of "Do people read literature?" we need to examine if it is worth the time, the reasons for readers' choices, the background needed to read and to understand literature, and finally, the requisites and obstacles readers need or face when reading literature.

Investing Time and Making Choices

We addressed the notion of it being worth the time in our previous discussion of the value of literature, what can be achieved through the reading of literature, and the goals it sets for reading instruction. Readers' reasons for their reading choices vary tremendously depending upon their age, their maturity, their intellectual ability, and their emotional dispositions. The choices may vary on the basis of personal interests in different activities and topics.

What people read can vary in terms of quality and taste. These variations in the choices of texts read shape the nature of the literary interactions between the reader and the text. The purposes for reading may influence whether or not people read a great deal, or periodically. Unfortunately, other activities compete for the time invested in reading literature. Considering how these activities influence the reading of literature may help to identify the reasons for not reading.

The Reasons for Not Reading Literature

A corollary question is "Why don't people read literature?" Some specific reasons come to mind. To name a few, because of time in general, because of competing activities, because of specific needs at different times, to satisfy different personal or professional needs, because books lack immediate relevance, or because they simply are too difficult to understand.

Often people simply choose to do other things such as playing tennis, joining social clubs, doing volunteer work, being involved in community activities, visiting friends, and other such activities. These activities take time, and interfere with people reading, or reading in more than a superficial way.

There also may be barriers to reading and understanding literature related to the reader's background. Certainly the difficulty of the material, especially when it isn't contemporary, or readers don't have the level of maturity needed for the concepts in the text is important. There is the possibility that the reader needs specific linguistic and cognitive ability such as the ability to process abstract language and thinking. Depending upon the book, there may be a need for some formal training in the literary aspects we presented earlier to do a literary reading of a book.

The reader's selection and judgment of a book may rest with their background, level of maturity, age, linguistic ability, or cognitive ability. In sum, we see there is a range and complexity of factors involved in a reader's ability to gain in-depth understanding when time for reflective reading has so many competing interests and intellectual requisites.

With some background established on literature, we move to the focus of this book—young adult literature. Here the question arises as to "What is young adult literature?" and "How does it fit into the literary landscape? In what ways does it help or enhance the reading experience of literature for young adults?" The next section of the chapter considers these concerns.

YOUNG ADULT LITERATURE

What Is the Nature of Young Adult Literature?

Answering these questions requires identifying the defining characteristics of young adult literature by giving its general characteristics, audience concerns, young adult issues, and topics relevant to young adult readers. The characteristics separate this literature from that written specifically for adult readers, yet, in some cases there is an overlap.

Nilsen and Donelson (2009) give us a useful list of seven characteristics for young adult literature that are helpful to selecting material for the young adult reader. We share them here, and make a further note of how they work for understanding the nature of young adult literature and as a guide for selecting books. Figure 1.7 combines these seven characteristics with additional explanation and several more characteristics that we think apply.

Identifying these characteristics as ones for young adult literature does not preclude them from being relevant to the adult reader; however, they do represent characteristics that tend to make a book more appealing to the young adult reader. To understand the relevance of these characteristics we turn to understanding the young adult audience.

Who Is The Audience?

We need to raise the question "How is the audience the primary distinguishing factor when defining young adult literature?" In considering this question we delineate the age range, factors in variations of the audience, general appeal, the concept of bridge books, themes, and problems and influences for change.

Ages

The audience is the primary defining characteristic of books for young adults. We expand the usual defined age to a range of eleven years to twenty-one years. This extends the usual age range by about three years because we believe that many young adults mature later because of an extended period of young adult dependency on others for different reasons. For some people this is arguable; but from our observations of many young people and the nature of the books written for young readers, we find that their experiences, even when they seem more extensive, do not always give them the emotional and cognitive development needed for many adult books. Many young adults often appear more "grown up" than they are.

Factors in Variation

The primary difference is its intended audience and how the themes of literature are transformed for the young adult audience. The next difference is the age of the characters and the conflicts and the problems that they face. Protagonists tend to be young adults facing the struggles of young adults. The third difference is simply an extension of the first two, and actually is

Characteristic 1	Writing from the viewpoint of young people. This helps the young adult reader enter the book at a level they can understand and makes them feel the author understands them
Characteristic 2	The young adult takes the credit for solving the problems. It is not the parent giving the young adult reader a sense of confidence and empowerment
Characteristic 3	The writing is fast – paced because the young adult readers are not usually reflective or patient, often they are impulsive and fast acting.
Characteristic 4	Inclusion of a variety of genres and subjects. This helps the young adult reader to see ideas and events in a variety of ways and to see those ideas and events presented differently
Characteristic 5	Stories about characters from many ethnic and cultural backgrounds should be included. This gives students an opportunity to learn about different ways of life
Characteristic 6	The stories are generally optimistic with characters making worthy accomplishments. This reinforces looking forward to the positive things in life
Characteristic 7	The writing deals with emotions that are important to young adults. This gives young adult readers some place to enter a book emotionally
Characteristic 8	The book makes a contribution to the growth of the young adult reader by serving a developmental purpose of moving the young adult to maturity
Characteristic 9	The book often depicts contemporary events or situations because it gives an understandable content and background for the young adult reader
Characteristic 10	The approach is one that is readable and understandable even when the conceptual content of the book is difficult and seemingly beyond the young adult reader because the author recognizes the linguistic and cognitive level of the reader
Characteristic 11	The language of the young adult book mirrors the language of the young adult, yet represents any well-written piece of literature and still recognizes the need for the familiarity of the language and concepts to process meaning
Characteristic 12	Various genres may help the reader see the same concept or issue in different ways by situating a problem in the appropriate genre to make it more interesting and accessible to the young adult reader

Figure 1.7. Characteristics of Young Adult Literature.

the mechanism for implementing them. That means that the themes from literature are presented with a different depth of complexity through the young adult protagonist, but still with the defining characteristics of the themes and problems identified later in this chapter.

The background experience of the young adult reader because of their specific life experiences may differ from that of the adult reader. This depends upon the roles that the young adult reader has had in their life. The nature of schooling and general intellectual ability may differ from the adult reader, and thus have an impact on the appropriateness of the book.

Using the young adult book may need a different approach to selecting and organizing what and how to use books for young adults. Themes and problem-orientation can be a useful organizing system for defining the curriculum for using books for young adults. Genre can be an organizer too. There also may be differentiation in terms of instructional approach and the need to motivate the young adult reader. Because of our concern with identity development, we will focus on themes and problems.

Author Concerns

To answer the question "How are authors influenced by audience?" we must consider how authors use the audience to guide their writing and to generate an appeal to the audience. Authors need to understand the range of differences within the young adult audience.

Sometimes authors find that the book has appeal to a range of audiences beyond even the differences within the young adult audience. Sometimes, although not intentionally, books bridge a gap between young adult readers and adult readers. This can be the case for books intended for the young adult audience or not.

We need to consider the economic and market influences factor into the decision to write for young adults. There also is the reality that there is a good market for books for young adults that may be a factor in choosing to do this kind of writing. Authors also may have personal experiences that translate well into books for young adults, and will sell easily given the scope of topics that are acceptable today.

Bridge Books

We believe that there is a category of books that we call "bridge books" that appeal to young adult readers and adult readers depending upon the developmental stage of the reader and the purposes for reading. We think that a "bridge book" stage has emerged with books intended for either young adult or adult audiences, but written with accessibility and interest for both groups of readers. These books may be the selections of "book clubs" and have a social purpose as part of the reading experience. They address important concepts and problems but with a style and emphasis on developing some of the outcomes of literacy we addressed earlier in this book.

In bridge books there is fluidness to the writing with a focus on the human element of living. They give vicarious experience, or expanded experience, and an understanding of the way people live different lives. These "bridge books" may work in two directions when selecting books for either audience. They may be a transition link from young adulthood to adulthood and the reading that many people do as they become lifelong readers.

Applying the themes to the selection and the instruction of young adult books gives the curriculum the basis for helping young adults understand concepts at their experiential and developmental level. Our belief is that it also prepares them for reading more complex, adult literature. This may be true of fiction or nonfiction, narratives or exposition. Adults simply may take away different understandings because of their experience.

What is clear is not that the books need to be immediately relevant but that the themes, issues, and problems can be made relevant to the young adult reader. In this book, we focus on themes issues and problems relative to identity because we believe identity formation is the key to the transformation that we see in young adults, and that will be of interest and helpful to them. Through these themes, books can be made relevant.

Themes and Problems: A Focus on Identity

It appears that the acceptable givens in our society have changed as society has been more open about previously unacceptable topics. This has given authors "permission" to address topics and themes in a different way than in the past. The themes and problems may be transformed for the young adult reader with sensitive topics that are not hidden from their view anymore. Wholesomeness is not a criterion for telling a story anymore.

In this book we select problems and themes related to the development of the young adult's identity. This answers the question "Who am I?," as this identity is rendered in various ways.

The chart that follows (figure 1.8) attempts to classify many of the problems by themes that young adults face. We then transform these problems via themes for selecting and organizing the books young adults may find relevant to answering the question of "Who am I?"

By identifying the problems of young adults, we can take the immediate concrete concerns of the young adult and classify them according to the themes that address these concerns in young adult books. This moves the thinking during reading and instruction to a more conceptual level.

These problems can be translated into themes for organizing the young adult's reading. These themes are the ones that we will use when developing some of the illustrative lessons later in this book and prepare the young reader for more complex literature. The four themes are as follows:

1. *Personal, social, and character identity*
2. *Losses and challenges that spur growth*
3. *General pressures and challenges*
4. *Focused identity development.*

We have focused on identity and growth in emotional and intellectual aspects of the young adult's development in this book because of the transformational aspect of young adult development. It is a stage of life where young people address the questions of who they are, what they want to do, and what they are capable of doing.

The answers to these questions often change later in life as an individual takes on new roles either in their personal or professional lives. Sometimes, with the help of reading this type of book young people develop a better perception of themselves and how other people see them.

Books for young adults can carry the reader through the life experiences of self and others to a state of maturity. The young adult learns to see situations through the eyes of others, and makes decisions with that understanding in mind. The question arises, "How is this a transformation?" and "Does it have to be difficult?"

Books can remove the problems from the self so that the reader sees characters handle problems and concerns as a way to develop understanding of the human dilemmas of the life experience. This type of reading can reduce the pain of growth by seeing the growth process through the book's story or exposition. In identifying, or not identifying, with the characters in the book, the reader shapes a sense of self.

If we can identify triggers for transformation, we may be able to select the appropriate books for groups of readers or for individual readers. If we look to personal life experiences we may be able to prompt and to understand their emotional development and behavior. If we look to their education, formal or informal, we may be able to shape or to understand their intellectual development.

We also need to consider how their immediate group affiliation shapes them and influences their growth and their goals in life. What may be helpful here is an understanding of the importance and the history of books for young adults and their place in various learning environments. The next section of this chapter addresses this concern.

THE IMPORTANCE OF YOUNG ADULT LITERATURE FOR YOUNG ADULTS

Young adult literature contributes to the development of identity and growth of the young adult by being part of their emotional, intellectual, and general development. In doing this, it transforms young adults in a volatile and transformational stage of developing as human beings. Often it is driven by their personal lives and the lives of their peers and others they know.

Personal, Social, and Character Identity			
Group A: The first three subgroups of problems are tied together as a theme of becoming a young adult by helping the young adult *establish a personal, character and social identity.*			
Defining One's Self	Integrity Concerns	Status and Roles in Life	
Autonomy Privacy Identity Being Cool Body Image Self-Worth Self-discovery Religious/spiritual self Sexual Orientation Gender Identity/Expression Race/Ethnicity Personal Abilities	Honesty Trust Courage	Relationships Peer Pressure Divorce Maturity	
Losses and Challenges that Spur Growth			
Group B: The second sub-group of problems expands on the concept of being a young adult by adding the dimension of the *losses and challenges that may spur growth and maturity.*			
Serious Situations	Personal Losses	Well-being and Health	
Rape Suicide Drugs Homelessness/poverty Being evicted Family member in jail Unexpected pregnancy	Loss of friends Death of Loved One	Illnesses Learning Disability Physical Differences/(Dis)abilities Mental Health	
General Pressures and Challenges			
Group C: The third group represents *general forces that put pressure and challenges* on young adults.			
Keeping Up with Demands		Facing Negative Forces	
World moves too fast Balance in life Materialism/ Money High Stakes Testing College concerns Sports		Social Media Cyberbullying School Violence Abuse Sexual Predators (online & offline)	
Focused Identity Development			
Group D: The fourth subgroup addresses the challenges and difficulties that the young adult faces and translates into establishing further specific aspects of identity related to *gender, sexual, ethnic, religious, political, ideological and occupational and status identity*			
Gender and Sexual identity	Identify, maintain or transform one's racial/ethnic, national or religious identity	Political/Ideological Identity	Occupational Identity and Status
Sex Gender Identity Gender Expression Sexual Orientation	Racial Identity(ies) Ethnic Identity(ies) Cultural values/beliefs Nationality(ies) National Identity(ies) Immigration Status Language(s) Religious Identity(ies)/Affiliations Religious values/beliefs	Political Party Affiliation Political/Ideological Values and Beliefs	Current Occupation and/or Future Occupational Goals Employed/Unemployed Eligibility to work

Figure 1.8. **Themes on Identity.**

In considering the contribution of books for young adults to human emotional and intellectual development we must consider the influences on identity and growth, transformations, and the role of life experiences.

For now, we turn to see how these books have gone through the historical transformation that makes them suitable for guiding the transformation and the development of the young adult reader's identity development.

HISTORICAL AND CONTEMPORARY CONTEXTS

The History of Young Adult Literature and Its Place in the Curriculum and in the Virtual Community

In considering the history and the evolution of books for young adults we examine the origins; the causal factors for change; and the relationships to identity, growth, and instruction.

Some of this discussion mirrors or extends the previous section's discussions.

Historical Origins: What Is the History and the Evolution of Young Adult Literature?

Mapping the historical origins of books for young adults may be a book in itself; however, we hope to give at least an overview of these origins as they have influenced the changes in the nature of books intended for young adults. To do this, we examine how they relate to use, popularity, and contribution to development from the 1500s forward by tracing and identifying the triggers for these origins and the changes that occurred (Owen, 2003).

A Brief Look Back at the Beginnings of Young Adult Literature

The themes and plots associated with books for young adults reverberate throughout the literature of the past. Shakespeare's *Romeo and Juliet* (1597) eloquently expresses the theme of young love pitted against the prejudices of rival families. In Jane Austen's *Emma* (1815) the reader listens as Austen, through the twenty-one-year-old narrator Emma, comments on the institution of marriage and the foolishness of societal conventions that present obstacles to open communication. In Charles Dickens's *Great Expectations* (1861), we meet Pip, a young man immersed in the web of love, social class, and morality. In *The Adventures of Huckleberry Finn* (1885), Mark Twain portrays the loneliness of a young boy, Huck Finn, who is abused by his father. The reader experiences the struggle Huck endures as he tries to understand the impact of the deep racist attitudes of the town.

Certainly these "coming of age" novels elucidate the themes still present in young adult literature today. However, although the themes of young adult literature have been present, for many young adults the style and the voice of the authors have not been easily accessible.

In many ways, the beginning of young adult literature as we know it today began in 1951 with the publication of J. D. Salinger's *The Catcher in the Rye*. Although it was initially published as an adult novel, teenagers were quickly drawn to it. In the voice of Holden Caulfield, the narrator, young adults heard their own voice, saw their own struggles, and felt their own fears. The themes in the novel, such as the protection of childhood innocence, the hypocrisy of "phoniness" of the adult world, the pain and sadness of growing up, alienation as a form of self-protection, the reality of death, and the confusion of sexual identity, have become themes commonly explored in books for young adults today.

Sixteen years later, in 1967, *The Outsiders*, the landmark "young adult" novel, was published. The author, S. E. Hinton, had begun writing the novel three years earlier when she was fifteen. In a 1981 interview with *Seventeen* magazine Hinton explains the reasons she felt compelled to write a novel that described the struggles of teens in a realistic way: "I'd wanted to read books that showed teenagers outside the life of 'Mary Jane went to the prom.' When I couldn't find any, I decided to write one myself. I created a world with no adult authority figures, where kids lived by their own rules." *The Outsiders* was a novel written "for teenagers, about teenagers, written by a teenager."

When *The Outsiders* was published, readers were shocked by the honest portrayal of teenagers smoking, drinking, and rumbling. Hinton's insightful novel about the conflicts between the Socs, or Socials, and Greasers became an immediate success and continues to be among the best-selling young adult novels of all time.

With *The Outsiders*, S. E. Hinton changed not only the way young adult fiction would be written but also the way young adult fiction would be read. Since the publication of *The Outsiders*, young people have demanded books that reflect the complexity and the reality of their lives. *The Outsiders* continues to influence the way young adult books are both read and written.

The late 1960s experienced a break with topics that were considered appropriate for teenagers. During this time books such as Ann Head's *Mr. and Mrs.*

Bo Jo Jones (1967), Paul Zindel's *The Pigman* (1968) and *My Darling, My Hamburger* (1969) dealt with issues such as gang warfare, teen pregnancy, and the challenges of African American youth.

Within the 1970s and early 1980s the genre continued to develop and it was in this decade many well-known authors such as Lois Duncan, Judy Blume, and Robert Cormier were publishing books. These writers were indicative of the commitment by many outstanding writers to speak to young adults with directness and honesty in a way in which young readers could relate. This period has been referred to as the golden age of young adult literature, when a highly intelligent and sophisticated literature was written for young people.

As might be expected, following the successes of the 1970s and early 1980s, during the mid-1980s and early 1990s young adult literature witnessed a period when publishers desired quantity over quality. During this time there was a proliferation of series books such as *Sweet Valley High* and *The Vampire Diaries*. These books were often predictable romance or grisly horror books and were considered inferior to previous books for young adults. This was a time when the educational research was reporting a decline in young people's desire to read and the government was instituting cuts to education funding. It seemed that the genre of young adult literature was at the point of dying out.

However, the past few decades have seen a resurgence in young adult literature. The 1990s books such as Lois Lowry's *The Giver* (1993), J. K. Rowling's *Harry Potter and the Sorcerer's Stone* (1997), Laurie Halse Anderson's *Speak* (1999), and Stephen Chobsky's *The Perks of Being a Wallflower* (1999) represent the sophisticated style as well as the range of topics explored by the writers of books for young adults.

During the decades following the 1990s, the topics include suicide, depression, gay love, violent acts, rape, trauma, vampires, murder, and concerns about society, such as the environment and economic equity and facial equity. As society pushes young people into adulthood faster, young adult books reflect this societal shift. Books such as John Green's *Turtles All the Way Down* (2017) as well as Ashley Hope Pérez's *Out of Darkness* (2012), Jenny Hubbard's *And We Stay* (2015), and Angie Thomas's *The Hate U Give* (2017) represent the relevance of current young adult literature as these books explore current topics such as anxiety, teen suicide, police violence on African American youth, and destructive racism.

The 2000s have seen writers explore more creative styles for their books for young adults. The style of writing varies across a whole spectrum and includes prose and poetry, realism and surrealism, objective and personal. The formats are varied and include verse, graphic novels, nonfiction accounts, movie scripts, picture books, and diaries.

With these developments young adult literature is becoming more accepted as a respected form of literature. It is critical that this high quality, sophisticated, rich, relevant literature is recognized, supported, and promoted within the lives of young adults.

In addition to identifying the origins and time frame for changes we consider the causal factors and the market forces at work with regards to these changes.

THE CAUSAL FACTORS: MARKET FORCES AND CHANGE OVER TIME

We need to identify specific causal factors and discuss their influence on the origins of various forms of young adult literature. Societal changes about givens and openness on topics may have had a considerable influence on the origins and acceptance of particular types of young adult books. Sometimes the books simply became more interesting to read as well as less condescending in tone and subject. Books started to "look the reader in the eye" and say what the author wanted to say. Whether the book simply has appeal to the young reader is a factor too. A focus on the themes identified here heightens this appeal. There are other factors too, such as market forces.

The Market Forces

Bookselling is an industry driven by economic conditions, specifically, who has the money to buy books, and what type of books do people buy for what purpose? The affluence of our society, and particularly of the young adult population, gives readers the money to purchase books.

The greater openness in society allows young adults to choose their own books and perhaps venture where they hadn't been in earlier times. Often large bookstores develop marketing strategies for selling books with or without regard for the quality of the book. "Can we still sell the classics? Are young adult books still "wholesome"? Should they be? Do the books have happy endings? Should they?" We don't really know all of the dimensions of answering these questions. Perhaps it may be helpful to sum up the changes over time to address the questions.

The Influence of Changes Over Time

We raise the question of "In what ways has young adult literature changed through the years?" and "What has influenced the changes?" We answered this question in one way in the previous section on the historical origins of young adult literature. In light of our discussion we think that young adult literature has grown up and also grown with the young adult reader.

Historically, we have seen changes in the substance of young adult books that reflect the depth of those factors that make the books for young adults more substantive, yet appropriate for contributing to the growth of the young adults. We also have seen that even where topics parallel those of adults, the approach may be different in the young adult book. The story or issue is now developed from a perspective more aligned with the psychological and sociological stage of young adulthood. The books also may be more influenced by trends in lifestyle to keep the themes and issues current and relevant to the young adult reader. This gives a good match to the reader's life experiences.

As the books available changed, and some of our understandings about the psychological and sociological concepts of young adulthood changed, we saw a greater acceptance of young adult literature in the classroom by teachers who started to recognize its value. These books then found a place in the classroom, or at least as independent reading for the young adult.

Many of the books lost the vapidness of early young adult books giving them more substance and appeal to both the young adult reader and the teachers who needed to choose books for readers of various abilities and inclinations with regards to reading in general. With these understandings came a rethinking of the use and the selection of young adult literature in the school curriculum.

In considering how young adult literature fits into aspects of schooling we examine its place in the schools with regards to instruction, independent reading, its advantages, and its accessibility and difficulty. We also consider the case against its use and any transformation caused by the virtual community.

WHAT IS ITS PLACE IN THE TRADITIONAL SCHOOL CURRICULUM?

The Regular Curriculum and Instruction

Once book selections are made with consideration for curriculum goals, the approaches to instruction can be decided. Depending upon how the curriculum is arranged, we may find these approaches vary not only with the curriculum but also with the type of student we will be teaching.

This book presents three specific approaches to instruction that can accommodate a variety of students, books, and goals and be incorporated into almost any curriculum. They are the Independent Instructional Unit (IIU), the mini-lesson, and the student-developed lesson. Each will be developed, explained, and illustrated in chapter 5 of this book. Here we may want to address some principles for instruction that guide the use of these approaches and help the reading of any type of book that is part of the regular curriculum.

Principles for Instruction and for Independent Reading

In any of the three approaches to instruction that may be incorporated into the regular curriculum and independent reading there may be some general principles that apply. We suggest the following:

1. *Why this book at this time in the reader's life?* This is an important question to ask when choosing books for either instructional purposes or independent reading.
2. *Can the reader be expected to interact with the book and gain meaning from the message?*
3. *Is there some preparation needed for instruction or an introduction to the book? What might it be? How do we accomplish it?*
4. *Is the teacher prepared adequately to guide the reading of the text?*

These questions and principles guide not only instruction but also the organization of the regular curriculum. The selection of books needs to be brought together not only with the themes but also with these principles in mind. The books need to connect to each other, not be taught or read as individual entities, and also must be made relevant and appropriate for the young adult reader.

Aside from choosing books for curricular and for instructional purposes, we need to consider the role of young adult books in independent reading. We do believe the same concerns as expressed in these four principles can serve as a guide.

Independent Reading

Young adult books may be useful as independent reading as a way to introduce readers to a variety of books as well as to encourage reading for pleasure and enlightenment. They can be offered to accommodate a range of reading abilities and interests as well as to introduce readers to types of books that they may not be familiar with reading. Using books for young adults this way removes the formality of reading for the teacher's goals, and allows the young adult reader to determine their own purposes and goals for reading what they choose to read.

Some of the principles for instruction identified in the previous section apply here too for guiding the selection and use of independent reading material. When young adult readers select books for independent reading there often is a concern about the quality and adherence to a limited number of genre. We believe that eventually this type of reading changes as young adult readers develop as individuals, and their life experiences change, and the reasons for reading change too. They either outgrow books that seem immature or of lesser quality, or learn to tackle more complex books as a result of class instruction and their own needs.

Simply allowing choice and reading for less than formal goals brings an element of appeal to the young adult's reading selections and habits. We also may learn more about our students by giving them the opportunity to explore new areas of interest, or become more knowledgeable about continuing areas of interest. These books can also prepare young adult readers for more difficult books that are part of the traditionally accepted books that are part of the regular school curriculum. Knowing the specific reading goals helps young adult readers and teachers to know when and what independent reading is useful immediately or as preparation for more complex books. Choosing books also can depend upon their accessibility and affordability.

The Influence of Accessibility and Affordability

What has happened to make these books accessible may be attributed to several things. First, the paperback and now the e-books have made books more affordable and portable in ways that encourage more reading. Second, the young adult reader has more income that is discretionary income. Third, authors can write books that are about more mature topics that young adult readers can buy with their discretionary money. With this accessibility and affordability we can encourage more reading.

The Quality and Difficulty of the Books

The question of literary merit always arises, and needs to be addressed. Our guess is that many adults are not reading other than the books on the best seller lists, and that they are reading more for pleasure and escape than for high-level enlightenment on serious topics.

We should not assume that all books for young adults do not have literary merit at a level that is appropriate for developing the skills and interests of young adult readers. Just looking to books that are endearing and universal for children, we see how books written for younger audiences have had an appeal and value for everyone. They are the books that have staying power. The same can be said about some young adult books.

In many ways young adult books are focused on the young adult audience so that the topics are both appropriate and relevant to the reader. Allowing exploration of these topics through independent reading often leads to reading more complex material at the right time in the young adult reader's life. The books for young adult readers tend to be at a more appropriate conceptual level of difficulty because the language and the structure of the book are appropriate for that audience.

These factors contribute to maintaining the motivation and the interest in reading the books. This can help contribute to the readers' growth and a personal identity at a transformative stage of life. All of these advantages can come without cost to the literary merit of a book and the ability to be used to focus on teaching with specific goals for reading in mind.

We think that it is important to keep in mind that sometimes readers just want something easy to read—plain and simple. We see this with the "bridge books" that we spoke of earlier where adults like books actually written for young adults, and that the easy-to-read books that are written for adults but with more sophisticated topics have appeal for the young adult reader. Transitions in either direction address the difficulty factor.

The Case against Its Use

There is the view, a legitimate one, that time not spent with more substantial books do not prepare young adults for further formal education. We think that the jury is still out on this view, particularly when the reader doesn't get much from the book. Is the time well spent if young readers trudge through a book that they don't understand? Or is more damage done to the incentive to develop lifelong readers? We address this concern more fully in chapter 2.

Finally, we need to consider the evolving nature of literacy by addressing the realities of a virtual community.

THE INTEGRATION INTO THE VIRTUAL COMMUNITY: WHAT IS ITS PLACE IN THE VIRTUAL COMMUNITY?

Defining the Virtual Community

Since the early days of the Internet, the formation of communities was central to its users. Even before American Online popularized chat rooms, early adopters connected digitally through Bulletin Board Systems. These asynchronous digital spaces allowed users to exchange information and connect with people around the world. As technology improved, these digital spaces morphed into real-time communities that allowed for synchronous virtual communication between two or more people anywhere in the world. Thus, virtual communities were born.

Because communities no longer necessarily consist of those who are nearest us geographically, but instead can be formed globally across digital platforms, there is a great opportunity to connect with people who have shared interests, beliefs, and values. In many instances, these virtual communities play a more significant role in our lives than the ones "in real life (IRL)." Connection to these digital spaces is widespread, with over 95 percent of all American teenagers reporting access to a smartphone (Anderson and Jiang, 2018).

According to the latest research from the Pew Research Center, today's teens "see digital environments as important spaces for youth to connect with their friends and interact with others who share similar interests. For example, 60% of teens say they spend time with their friends online on a daily or nearly daily basis, and 77% say they spend time in online groups and forums" (Anderson and Jiang, 2018).

It is important to note that the study does not make clear the definitions of "friends," meaning it is possible teens lump their online and offline friends into the same category, making it difficult to discern which of those friends they are spending time with online. In many instances, teens interact with their geographically adjacent friends online as much as they do offline. It is precisely this behavior that injects credence into the idea that virtual communities can be harnessed for learning in the classroom. These digital spaces are both familiar and comfortable for teenagers, making them excellent places to explore the sensitive and difficult topics often associated with young adult literature in both synchronous and asynchronous formats.

The Integration of Literature and the Virtual Community

Though many teachers are hesitant to embrace virtual communities, and may dismiss them as nonacademic space, we cannot ignore their influence. We are living in a time when many people get their news from tweet, read and write literature on Medium, or download the latest best-selling book onto their e-reader. It is important that teachers explicitly incorporate the virtual community into reading literature. We need to tap its usefulness as a teaching and a learning resource.

SUMMING UP

Chapter 1 has helped us to understand the nature and the value of literature in general as well as the importance of young adult literature for young readers. The chapter also has introduced us to three significant perspectives: the literary, the psychological, and the sociological views that support our choice to focus on how books for young adults can contribute to the transformative nature of the young adults' development, personally and intellectually. The chapter focused on how this transformation shapes the young adults' growing sense of identity.

Chapter 2

Theoretical Perspectives on the Literary, Psychological, and Sociological Aspects of Young Adults' Identity and Growth

OVERVIEW OF CHAPTER 2

Chapter 2 directs our attention to the theoretical underpinnings of what we have said already and to what we will illustrate in subsequent practically oriented chapters. The three theoretical perspectives addressed here are literary, psychological, and sociological ones because they help understand the identity and the growth of young adults as these concepts relate to aspects of using young adult literature and developing skill in lifelong reading.

In considering the transactional view of literature and its implications we consider Rosenblatt's work, the application of Rosenblatt, reading literature for its own sake as well as the implications for instruction, the nature of finding meaning, and the role of life and literary experiences. We consider literary reading principles for instruction, themes that drive instruction, integration of themes of identity and growth, and the expected outcomes of reading literature and the role of teachers in developing the abilities of young adult readers. Some of the discussion overlaps and extends the ideas presented in chapter 1.

In considering the psychological perspectives we examine defining the transformative years and the formation of identity, defining the self, important developmental tasks, conflict and struggles, indicators of growth, and reading maturity to develop lifelong readers. Here we consider the views of specific psychologists and the relationships to instructional goals and the themes presented in chapter 1. We concern ourselves with psychological development because reading literature is first an individual task before it becomes a shared activity. The same can be said for young adults. They are at once separate and onto themself before being part of a larger group of other young adults.

In considering the sociological perspectives, we review the theories of major contributors to the development of young adults by examining group affiliation; peer, environmental, and emotional pressure; self-perception; and support systems. These factors contribute to our understanding of young adults' identity beyond individual identity to interactions with others and broader settings. These three theoretical perspectives come together to help us shape our views of the young adult and their impact on the reading of young adult literature.

QUESTIONS GUIDING THE READING

What is the transactional view of literature and its implications and applications for reading literature?

How does the Continuum of Engagement, Transaction, and Understanding Model help us with understanding the transactional view of literature?

What are the expected outcomes that can be derived from this literary perspective?

Who are the key contributors to the psychological and sociological theory on young adult development?

What is the significance of the themes of identity and growth in the work presented here?

What are the challenges of identity development in the transformative years of young adulthood?

What is the effect of facing these challenges on reading young adult literature?

What is the influence of group affiliation, peer and environmental pressure, and self-perception on the development of young adults?

What are the sociological support systems for young adults?

LITERARY PERSPECTIVE

Louise Rosenblatt's Theory of Aesthetic Reading: The Critical Component of Engagement

> *We peel off layer after layer of concerns brought to bear—social, biographical, historical, linguistic, textual—and at the center we find the inescapable transactional events between texts and readers.*
>
> *—The Reader, The Text, The Poem, 1978, p. 175*

More than eight decades ago the literary theorist Louise Rosenblatt warned that teachers were failing to develop students' ability to respond aesthetically to literature. Rosenblatt felt that "aesthetic reading, by its very nature, has an intrinsic purpose, the desire to have a pleasurable, interesting experience for its own sake" (Rosenblatt, 2005, p. 83). This same warning is extremely relevant to our current educational climate in which teachers are required to emphasize standardized testing at the cost of the development of students' aesthetic experience.

Rosenblatt believed that this ability was essential to achieving the goal of producing a literate population who could participate fully in a thriving democracy. In her seminal work, *Literature as Exploration*, Rosenblatt (1995) suggests that "literary experiences might be made the very core of the kind of educational process needed in a democracy" (p. 261).

Clearly, Rosenblatt (1995) views the development of the aesthetic response critical not only to the individual's development but also to the continuation of the ideals of a democratic society. As students learn to participate actively in the reading of literature by experiencing the text, reflecting on its meaning, and deepening their responses through discussion, they are simultaneously developing a sensitivity to the needs of others, as well as a capacity to envision solutions to the challenging problems of living in a complex, diverse society.

The power of an aesthetic, personal experience lies in its potential to connect students' interests, emotions, and imagination with their intellect. Through literature, students can develop the ability to read in a thoughtful way that contains both an emotional and an imaginative quality critical in a democratic society. "Such sensitivity and imagination are part of the indispensable equipment of the citizens of a democracy" (Rosenblatt, 1995, p. 261).

Rosenblatt states that through literature "we participate in imaginary situations, we look on at characters living through crises, and we explore ourselves, and the world about us" (Rosenblatt, 1995, p. 37). Rosenblatt espouses that the reader is the center of the reading process and that each and every student can create a unique understanding of a text. Her theories encourage a belief that each student should have the opportunity to explore literature to develop a voice in the classroom and a voice in society.

Current books, newspapers, journal articles, and research summaries communicate a reality that conveys students' disenchantment with reading. The reasons for this are complicated, and contributing issues such as race, class, poverty, and equity are exceedingly complex. Yet, educators must understand that they will successfully meet the great challenges of helping those who need them most only if their instruction has a dual focus: teachers must teach children the skills necessary to access the texts they present, and they must simultaneously present works of literature in a way that will engage students in thought, emotion, and dialogue.

This type of engagement will lead students to experience literature with reciprocity of experience: students will bring a range of emotions to literature and often discover many of those same emotions unfolding in literature in a myriad of ways.

As students from middle schools and high schools experience literature, the experience leads them ultimately to explore themselves and society. Rosenblatt's theories reclaim the primary importance of the experiential dimension of reading prior to teaching literary devices and strategies. As Rosenblatt (1995) states, "All the student's knowledge about literary history, about authors and periods and literary types, will be so much useless baggage if he has not been led to seek in literature a vital personal experience" (p. 59).

This does not mean that such knowledge is not important; however, it has its place in enhancing the reader's experience with literature. It needs to be addressed at the appropriate time and place in the teaching and the use of literature in a reader's life and reading experiences. First, the reader must be engaged in the text at the personal level, and perhaps emotional level, so that they can move further to a deeper literary experience, perhaps at a formal, intellectual level. Second, the teacher can build upon the personal, aesthetic reading to develop the more highly conceptualized literary aspects of the text. Doing so helps the reader find meaning in the text.

TWO WAYS OF READING: THE AESTHETIC AND THE EFFERENT STANCE

Rosenblatt (1978, 1995) emphasizes that the meaning of a text is neither totally in the reader nor totally in the text, but rather in the transaction between the reader and the text. Rosenblatt (1995) contends that understanding how attention is focused illuminates whether the reading is aesthetic or efferent.

In efferent reading, "our attention is primarily focused on selecting out and analytically abstracting the information or ideas or directions for action that will remain when the reading is over" (p. 32). Generally speaking, while one is reading a factual text, the reader's focus is on information that can be recalled after the reading. Rosenblatt chose the term "efferent" to embody the meaning of the Latin word *effere*: to carry away.

The focus of the attention is quite different in aesthetic reading. This type of reading is generally associated with the reading of fiction. In aesthetic reading, instead of focusing attention on facts and ideas that will be used after the reading, the reader's attention is focused on what is being lived through at the moment. From this mixture of "sensations, feelings, images and ideas, is structured the experience that constitutes the story or poem or play" (Rosenblatt, 1995, p. 33). The greater proportion of attention is given to the private emotions, associations, ideas, and feelings that the text evokes.

Rosenblatt is clear that both stances can be applied to the same text. It is the reader's intention that determines the focus. The distinction is not one of active versus passive reading. In both stances, the reader is actively involved. In efferent reading, the reader approaches the text as a source of information; in aesthetic reading, the reader enters the text as a creative partner.

The teacher helps students become thoughtful, skilled readers by teaching them the different ways of reading a text, and various ways to get deep meaning from the text, whether it be fiction or nonfiction. Rosenblatt's criticism continues to resonate today; schools often emphasize efferent reading and sometimes neglect aesthetic reading. Oftentimes, this leads to losing the "lived-through" transactional experience of reading. This often leads to losing the "spirit" of the text.

With the development of aesthetic and efferent reading, we enhance an emotional and an intellectual response in reading literature. The development of emotion, a greater sense of self-knowledge, and an increased capacity for intellectual knowledge all contribute to developing a strong sense of identity. It represents the core of some of our thinking.

THE IMPLICATIONS OF DEVELOPING EMOTIONAL AND INTELLECTUAL READINGS FOR YOUNG ADULT LITERATURE

The enhancement of an ability to do an emotional and an intellectual reading helps the young adult reader reach the in-depth meaning that we strive for in both a personal and a literary reading of a book of any genre. This means that the young adult reader can respond and does respond with some degree of empathy and understanding to the human dilemmas or simple problems that the characters in any book face.

The young adult reader grows personally from having read the book and understanding the author's message to the fullest. The young adult reader then is capable of a rich interpretation of the book without straying from the author's purpose for writing the book. Developing this level of reading opens the door for the reader's self-exploration and intellectual growth.

Oftentimes when students "live-through" a literary work, emotional energy occurs within a framework of conflict. Rosenblatt (1995) points out that this emotional response is beneficial in the formation of identity. She reiterates John Dewey's idea that "rationality does not exist in opposition to emotion but rather represents the attainment of a working harmony among diverse desires" (p. 227). This process becomes evident when students experience emotional tension relating to the complex behavior of literary characters.

Literature gives students an opportunity to acknowledge, discuss, and respond to an emotionally charged literary context and to consider alternative behaviors through rational thinking. Rosenblatt stresses that literature itself and the discussions that follow may later be assimilated into actual behavior.

When a teacher combines the reader's emotional response to literature with the discussion of a broader response to the literature at hand, there is great potential not only for learning but also for action. The classroom environment in which students can exchange ideas and perspectives can contribute to the way students can assimilate ideas into actual behaviors and into their identities.

Reading as an Experience for Self-Exploration

The reading of a text presents a student with the opportunity for self-discovery. Through reading, discussion, and consideration of varying perspectives and different values, students are able to gain insight into their identity, a major concern of this book's message. Literature provides students with the potential to examine their own lives, and simultaneously gain insight into who they are and who they want to become.

Reading has the potential to change the young adult reader, and students need these opportunities to grapple with stories in a way that helps them evaluate attitudes, values, actions, and decisions.

Rosenblatt places this personal response to texts as paramount in the reading process. Rosenblatt (1978) explains, "No one else can read a text for him. He may learn indirectly about other's experiences with the text; he may come to see his own reading was confused or impoverished, and he may be stimulated to call forth from the text a better poem but this he must do himself" (p. 105).

Spontaneous and Personal Responses Lead to Intellectual Rigor and Growth

Although Rosenblatt (1978, 1995) reiterates many times that personal experience is paramount in reading fiction, she also emphasizes that this first, personal, aesthetic, spontaneous response should be the "first step toward increasingly mature responses" (1995, p. 71). She stresses that the goal of studying literature is not simply to offer a random emotional response, but rather to "give the student the form of emotional release that all the arts offer, and, at the same time, help him gain more complex satisfactions from literature" (p.71).

Through class discussions students will hear a range of responses that will lead them back to the text for a closer examination, and this closer scrutiny may lead the reader to a reformulation of the initial response. Rosenblatt (1995) believes the power of exchanges and discussions is that they lead to a scrutiny of responses and a deeper understanding of the texts.

As students articulate their ideas, they generate questions, return to the text for clarification, and consider the comments of their classmates. Then they will not only reformulate their response but also "develop ability to handle more and more demanding texts" (p. 272). There is room for engagement and reflection of the text. Clearly, this process lies at the heart of intellectual growth and identity formation.

Role of the Teacher

The challenge for teachers is to create an atmosphere where students can share their ideas, listen to varying perspectives, consider differing views, and gain insight into the literary work, themselves, and others. The teacher plays a critical role in creating such an atmosphere. Rosenblatt (1995) delineates the many responsibilities of the teacher:

> A situation conducive to free exchange of ideas by no means represents a passive or negative attitude on the part of the teacher. To create an atmosphere of self-confident interchange the teacher must be ready to draw out the more timid students and to keep the more aggressive from monopolizing the conversation. He must be on the alert to show pleased interest in comments that have possibilities and to help students clarify or elaborate their ideas. He must keep the discussion moving along consistent lines by eliciting the points of contact between different students' opinions. His own flexible command of the text and understanding of the reading skills it requires will be called into play throughout. (p.71)

Clearly, analysis of the text shouldn't eclipse the personal response, but rather respect each personal response as the crucial point of entry that has the potential to generate discussions that value ambiguity, questioning, and multiple interpretations. Our concern here is that we are losing the art of reading literature, and reading it well and to its fullest potential. One may ask, "Does it matter?" We believe that it does matter because reading literature is a fulfillment of getting to the deepest meanings of the human condition (Sumatra, 2002).

Contributions of Louise Rosenblatt to Teaching Young Adult Literature

Each time a teacher asks a student "What does this text mean to you?," Tell me what you think the story means?," or "Share your ideas about this piece of literature" they are inviting the students to embrace the power of individual, personal interpretation. Each time a teacher replaces worksheets and workbooks with genuine literature and authentic discussion, they are inviting students to participate in the power of stories. Each time a teacher encourages students to consider multiple perspectives and differing views, they are issuing a call for the students to participate in a democratic forum through which all students' voices are heard and respected.

Each time a teacher facilitates a discussion in which students are engaged in open-ended discussions, Louise Rosenblatt's staunch belief in the power of literature to nurture a critical citizenry lives on. Rosenblatt's theories and ideas are particularly relevant to young adults as they strive to develop their own voices, identities, and place within society.

Rosenblatt's own words in *Making Meaning with Texts* (2005) capture the far-reaching effect she has had on the teaching of literature as a means to simultaneously develop each individual's voice and the voice of democracy:

> Traditional teaching methods, passed on from generation to generation, were, I felt, producing shallow and unquestioning readers who passively accepted the authority of the printed word. . . . It seemed that students could be helped to develop the ability to read independently, purposefully, and critically. . . . Fostering a critical approach to all writings, no matter what their point of view, would in itself, I believe, serve the advancement of Democracy. (p. ix)

As a way of drawing together what we have drawn from Rosenblatt, we propose the following model (figure 2.1) to illustrate the components of the process of reading literature including young adult literature.

A MODEL: THE CONTINUUM OF ENGAGEMENT, TRANSACTION, AND UNDERSTANDING

Illustrating some of these ideas and how they address the question of "Where does meaning reside?" is the key to reading literature and specifically young adult literature. We look to framing these ideas in a simple model that combines the idea of a continuum of meaning with the construct of entry and engagement, transaction, and message and understanding with a literary text. The model considers the need for finding meaning through in-depth reading, engagement, and reflection. We will try to illustrate this in a simple visual and explanation of the components of the model.

Interaction of Levels A, B, and C

The model attempts to identify the levels of reading that the reader must draw into and from for engagement, transaction, and understanding to occur in any given reading of a text. The response to the question "Where does meaning reside?" asks the reader to integrate the processes involved at each of these

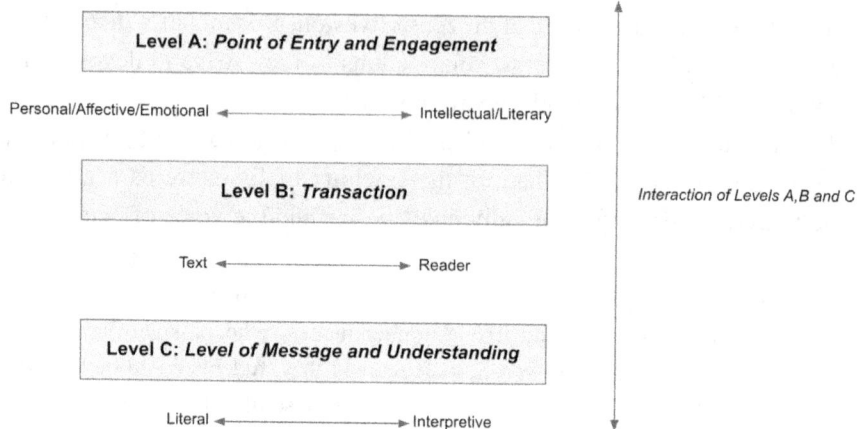

Figure 2.1. The Model: Continuum of Engagement, Transaction, and Understanding.

levels with the reader's purpose for reading to be met as the meaning of the text for a given reader is directed by those purposes and what the reader brings to the text.

With regards to the young adult reader, their immediate concerns, as reflected in the problems and themes they are preoccupied with, influence what occurs in bringing the three levels together to show what the meaning is that they get from the text. This is a complex synthesis process that is central to a good reading of literature. To clarify, let us look at each level independently and then their interactive states.

Components of the Model

Purpose—Sets the direction of reading and the point of entry and engagement, emotional and intellectual, as well as the type of transactions and understanding that emerge in the reading.

Interaction—The process of exchange across the three levels.

LEVEL A—*POINT OF ENTRY AND ENGAGEMENT*

"At what point personally and intellectually does the reader enter the text?" Addressing this may depend upon the purpose for reading as well as the general disposition to the book and the cognitive ability of the reader. "What is the reason for reading? What is their ability to understand the conceptual level of the essence of the text? How much time and energy are they willing to give to the text to make meaning from it? Is it being read for pleasure or for literary merit? Has the reader been prepared to read at both a personal and an intellectual level? Should instruction begin at one point rather than another? How is this decision made?"

How and where the reader enters and engages in the text is crucial to the reader's ability to experience a meaningful reading of the text. If the reader is entering the text at different points on the Level A continuum the reading experience can differ drastically. If the reader enters the text at the wrong point little or no meaning will be gained.

LEVEL B—*TRANSACTION*

How the author of the text and the reader construct intent and meaning addresses the issue of how much "deep sustained reading" will occur. Sometimes, it takes more than one reading to break through the literal expression to arrive at the interpretation of a text. The transaction represents the means to the outcome of understanding.

It is the interchange between the reader and the text that brings the reader's background to the text to create meaning. The entry/engagement driven by the purpose for reading will influence the nature and perhaps the fluctuating transaction between the text and the reader. The reader's life and educational experience may influence the transactions.

LEVEL C—*MESSAGE AND UNDERSTANDING*

One could say that most reading of literature is interpretative given what we understand about a reader's background and purpose for reading. Rosenblatt's view that the text is the stimulus for getting meaning influences the degree of interpretation derived from the reading. Also, the age of the reader and that reader's life experiences or education helps the reader to know at what level they should read the text.

One must determine a minimum literal level of meaning to maintain the integrity of the text and also to support any interpretation of the text. The readers' movement may fluctuate between a literal and interpretative meaning of the text based upon the interaction of Level A and Level B. Here is where meaning resides. It appears that most reading of literature is at some level of interpretation.

Interaction of A, B, and C or Some Combination

How the reader moves through the three levels, or some combination of them, drives the process of reading and the outcome of the reading. The question is "What does the reader take to the transaction to help them engage, reflect, and do the in-depth reading to finding the meaning of a text?" We ask three key questions here that we hope have been addressed by the model presented, and guide our use of literature in our own reading as well as our students' reading:

1. *Where do we find the meaning of the text?*
2. *Are we reading for in-depth meaning?*
3. *Are engagement and reflection a goal in our reading and instruction?*

THE ROLE OF LIFE AND LITERARY EXPERIENCES: WHAT THE READER TAKES TO THE TEXT

The role of life as an influencing factor is hard to determine because the reader may not even be aware of its influence. Some life experiences may be buried in each reader's subconsciousness. Such experience may not be visible to anyone guiding instruction either. The reader's literary experiences may be more visible because of the formal and intellectual language being used by the reader. In either case, it is hard to identify the impact or application of either factor on the reading of a text. For the young adult reader the problems and the themes of identity as presented in chapter 1 are key to the transaction. This may be because they represent the triggers for transformation of the young adult reader that are a part of being able to read appropriate young adult literature.

The Integration of Themes of Identity and Growth

The themes and the concrete problems related to these themes are reflective of the identity development and the transformative growth of the young adult as presented in psychological and sociological theory. They are the key to transaction. This focus is the concept driving the thinking and application of what we say here to instruction and in later chapters on instruction and assessment.

The Themes that Drive Transactions and Instruction

In chapter 1 we identified four major themes that may help organize our understanding of young adult development and guide instruction as well. We repeat them here as a refresher.

1. *Personal, social, and character identity*
2. *Losses and challenges that spur growth*
3. *General pressures and challenges*
4. *Focused identity development*

These themes suggest a focus for selecting books for instruction that will be meaningful to the young adult reader. They can be developed at a level and in such a way to engage the young adult reader without being limited in depth conceptually. There is adequate substance in the text for appropriate and meaningful instruction. They are almost guaranteed to trigger engagement at some level. However, they do rely on actual principles of instruction as noted earlier.

THE PRINCIPLES OF INSTRUCTION FOR GUIDING BOTH A PERSONAL AND A LITERARY READING

In addition to having a concern about levels of interaction in reading literature as reflected in the model just presented, we need to consider the principles of instruction that help us to teach these aspects in ways that enhance the young adult reader's obtaining meaning and depth of understanding. What we are aiming for here is understanding both the broad principles and the concrete elements of literary concerns as a reciprocal relationship of literary development and instruction. We identified four principles earlier, and would like to expand on that here. As a reminder, the four principles are as follows:

1. Why this book at this time in the reader's life? This is an important question to ask when choosing books for either instructional purposes or independent reading.
2. Can the reader expect to interact with the book and gain meaning from the message?
3. Is there some preparation needed for instruction for introducing the book? What might it be? How do we accomplish it?
4. Is the teacher prepared adequately to guide the reading of the text?

We propose these principles as a part of the means to reaching an in-depth understanding of the themes embedded in the books that young adult readers read.

Although literary concerns are at the core of guiding instruction for reading literature, they need to be preceded by the personal entry to a book. Then literary concerns can set the focus of instruction on aesthetic, emotional, personal, and intellectual response to any discussion by students, or any objective in a teacher's lesson.

In this book, we also tie this concern and the four principles to the themes of identity and growth because of our concerns with the development of young adults with literature as a venue for aiding this goal.

We hope to develop a framework that encompasses the parallel of young adult development and the development of the essence of the books that we are teaching. This allows young adult readers to bring their own experience and background to the books that they read, and at the same time move them beyond their own stage of development. The research in reading supports and provides strong evidence that various aspects of background, both life experience and knowledge of literary aspects of writing, influence how a reader approaches the reading along with how well they understand what they read.

Teachers have a significant role in accomplishing the goal of developing this reciprocal relationship so that young adults continue their future reading with the ability to integrate literary aspects of reading without overintellectualizing their reading of a text with this personal response. Our hope is that we can illustrate ways for the teacher to accomplish this goal in later chapters of this book.

THE EXPECTED OUTCOMES OF LITERACY RELATIVE TO LITERATURE

We continue and end this discussion on both personal and literary concerns by coming full circle to the outcomes of literacy identified earlier to show how they are compatible with Rosenblatt's views on literature and reading literature. The ultimate goal being the creation of young adult readers who can function in a democratic society in an intelligent and thoughtful way to develop aspects of the outcomes of literacy as presented in The Outcomes of Literacy Model (figures 1.5 and 1.6) and The Model of Continuum of Engagement, Transaction, and Understanding (figure 2.1).

As young adults address some of the issues in their lives and resolve any conflicts in those resolutions we will see them answering the question "Who Am I Becoming?" Their personal identity will be shaped and growth will have occurred. The hope is that through the literature that they read young adults are helped to achieve the outcomes of literacy as they answer the question of "Who are they becoming and where do they belong in this world?"

The next questions that follow this general discussion of Rosenblatt are "How important are literary concerns in reading literature? What is a 'literary reading' of a text? Is there a right way to read literature? Or are there many ways to read literature? Does knowledge of literary aspects of literature enhance the reading of the text beyond the personal, aesthetics of reading literature? How does all of this influence instruction of literature and the development of literary language?"

DEFINING A LITERARY READING: THE INTELLECTUAL EXPERIENCE

One way to define a literary reading of a text is to examine how specific literary aspects of literature, such as understanding figurative language, enhance the reading of the text. Generally, this means understanding how simile, metaphor, alliteration, personification, plot, theme, symbols, and internal structure such as flashback, denouement, climax, and the style of writing shape the meaning of the text. It means that we bring the knowledge of these aspects of literature to bear on the reading that we do either through analysis or as a result of having assimilated their role and nature related to literature.

We identified these aspects of literature earlier, and ask the reader of this book to recall them here. The application of these aspects of reading literature heightens the beauty of the language that carries the meaning of a text. By secondary school, instruction in these aspects should have happened so that the young adult reader can enhance a personal reading of the text.

We recognize that what we espouse in this book is not the only view of using literature at the secondary level; however, we think that for many young adults it is the most fruitful one. Too many young people leave their experience with reading literature more impoverished than enriched, and often don't continue to read more complex literature. We hope for better with our approach.

VIEWS OTHER THAN ROSENBLATT—HOW DO THEY FIT?

Are there other views and dimensions?
What are the other views for young adult literature?
What are the specific concerns derived from the other views?

Are literary concerns only intellectual and only based on a "literary reading" of the work? To address these questions we need to examine what an alternative view for reading literature would be. How does it fit with Rosenblatt? Or extend the overall view? Doing this gives balance to our discussion and acknowledges a different perspective. We also recognize that other views may dominate instruction in the schools now.

Of primary concern is a view that a piece of literature also conveys a literary type of writing and message agreed upon through a consensus of literary experts—that is, the "real meaning" lies in the text, and thus it is not a transactional process where the reader's background and experience shape the meaning derived from the text. In this view, the consensus of experts also agrees on the intent of the text, and that most literary concerns are intellectual ones (Richard, 1929).

This opposing view leads to more of a "right-wrong" mentality with regards to interpretation of the text meaning. Here we see that the meaning is in the text. It often focuses on teaching the intellectual aspect of response where structural and literary aspects of literature take center stage in instruction. This does not mean that the emotional aspect of reading literature is of no concern, just that it is not the focus of instruction. It is the "literary reading of a text" that drives instruction.

What is interesting is that even the "experts" often disagree on the intent of the author and the meaning of text. What then? Entering the text at the level of an intellectual reading requires a plethora of abilities, knowledge, and dispositions that still may be developing in the young adult reader. This complex of skills is variable with both the reader and the text.

Whether we adhere to Rosenblatt's transactional view or to an alternative view of the process of reading literature, we need to consider psychological and sociological underpinnings of development as they apply to young adult readers. These concepts are at the heart of identity development in general as well as for the young adult. We begin with psychological perspectives and then move to sociological ones in the next two sections of this chapter.

PSYCHOLOGICAL PERSPECTIVES

Defining the Transformative Years: Influences, Problems, and Issues—A Focus on Identity

The focus on identity and growth is our primary concern for the transformative years in young adult development. The psychological literature shows how a sense of one's identity begins forming early in life and changes as we assume new and different roles in our lives.

The literature suggests that growth and identity, although very much intertwined, are not exactly the same constructs. Growth reflects a process that leads to the establishment of one's identity. This growth occurs in developmental stages that have specific characteristics. This growth reflects one aspect of this movement toward establishing an identity and reaching maturity.

One's identity usually is dependent upon one's sense of self-perception as well as how other people see them. We explore this thinking, and then ask "Why is identity—of young adults in psychology and in literature—relevant as a focus for organizing reading and instruction of young adult literature? Why is it important?" Some of the answers to these questions lie in the idea that in growth, we see some struggling and confusion, where choices must be made that clarify and solidify one's identity. This growth reflects the changes in young adults' thinking that can come from reading and also enhance a young adult reader's literary understanding of text.

To address this concept we need to address the following questions: "What is identity development in young adulthood?" "What are the indicators of growth? How is it seen in young adults? How does it show taking responsibility? Who writes about identity? What do they say? What characterizes growth? Are the effects of growth both affective and intellectual?" Addressing these questions guides the discussion in this section of chapter 2.

The Psychological Challenges of Identity Development for Young Adults: Key Contributors

The focus here is on the psychological perspectives of young adult development with the emphasis on identity and growth in a transformative stage of development. Three psychologists are considered when exploring this psychological perspective. The first is Havighurst (1956), the second one is Erikson (1968), and the third one is Marcia (1980). Each approaches the concepts differently, but together they give us a timeless construction for understanding the young adult in relationship to young adult literature.

In chapter 1 we identified a number of problems that we think, and that young adults think, young adults face during young adulthood. These problems can be transposed into viable themes for organizing instruction in young adult literature as was presented earlier in chapter 1. Here we delineate some of the ideas presented in the work of psychological theorists that give us the underpinnings of the themes and problems we presented in chapter 1.

In general these ideas may be seen as developmental tasks or stages. As each of life's developmental tasks are resolved there usually is some growth that occurs for each young adult. Often this growth involves stabilizing key relationships in one's life and taking on new roles and responsibilities. In doing so, their sense of identity is shaped. To address this concern we examine these three psychologists and their views.

The three psychologists, Havighurst, Erikson, and Marcia, represent shifts and varying perspectives on young adult development that are germane to our understanding of the development of identity and growth in young adults. In turn, this influences our concerns with teaching young adult literature. They help us see the movement toward stabilizing key relationships as part of young adults' identity development.

Havighurst: A Historical View and His Developmental Tasks

Havighurst is the first of the psychologists we consider to address the psychological perspective on young adult development that we think may influence the reading of literature. His ideas on developmental tasks are given here as a basis for markers of growth in young adulthood that underlie and are aligned with some of the themes and problems that we identified in chapter 1. The limitation of Havighurst's original work is that it focused primarily on males. However, with refinement and adjustments there seems to be applicability to females. In any case, the developmental tasks that he identified have given us some theoretical base for our discussion in chapter 1 and the application of our thinking in later chapters.

Building on research and theories developed in the 1930s and 1940s Havighurst refined the notion of the developmental task, which he defined as follows: "a task which arises at or about a certain period in the life of the individual, successful achievement of which leads to his happiness and to success with later tasks, while failure leads to unhappiness in the individual, disapproval by society and difficulty with later tasks" (Havighurst, 1956).

For Havighurst, "When the timing is right, the ability to learn a particular task will be possible (Emphasis mine). This is referred to as a *teachable moment*. It is important to keep in mind that unless the time is right, learning will not occur. Hence, it is important to repeat important points whenever possible so that when a student's *teachable moment* occurs, she or he can benefit from the knowledge" (Havighurst, 1956).

Although Havighurst developed his ideas some time ago, they still have viability today with some modification. The developmental tasks are as follows:

Achieving new and more mature relations with age mates of both sexes
Achieving a masculine or feminine social role
Accepting one's physique and using the body effectively
Achieving emotional independence of parents and other adults
Preparing for marriage and family life
Acquiring a set of values and an ethical system as a guide to behavior
Desiring and achieving socially responsible behavior
Selecting and preparing for an occupation
Achieving assurance of economic independence

Although not necessarily intended as a hierarchical model, implicit in the list is a progression over time to accomplish each of the tasks. This set of developmental tasks has been translated into key problems and themes that were identified in chapter 1. We use them to guide the selection of books and the related instruction of young adult literature. This is one way of examining young adult development that has relevance for teaching young adult literature.

Next we see Erikson and Marcia address young adult development differently through stage models of development. In both cases we again see the concerns with identity at the core of young adult development.

Erikson: Eight Stages of Man—A Focus on Ego Identity and Role Confusion

Erikson (1968) gives us a good theoretical perspective on adolescent growth toward developing a sense of identity. A summary of this thinking follows here.

Most famous for expanding Freud's Theory of Psychosexual Stages, Erikson developed what he termed "The Eight Stages of Man." They are as follows:

1. *Infant (zero to one) trust versus mistrust*
2. *Toddler (two to three) autonomy versus shame and doubt*
3. *Preschooler (three to six) initiative versus guilt*
4. *School-Age Child (seven to twelve) industry versus inferiority*
5. *Adolescence (twelve to eighteen) ego identity versus role confusion*
6. *Young Adult (twenties) intimacy versus isolation*
7. *Middle Adult (late twenties to fifties) generativity versus self-absorption*
8. *Old Adult (fifties and older) integrity versus despair*

Key to our understanding of young adults and relevance to this work is Stage 5 as it is explained here. Stage 6 also presents some concerns for the young adult population, but not as much as Stage 5. In Stage 5 Adolescence (twelve to eighteen) we see a focus on resolving conflict related to role confusion as part of the growth process to establishing ego identity. This stage in Erikson's model occurs during young adulthood (for him twelve to eighteen years). At this time, young adults search for a sense of self and personal identity through an intense exploration of personal values, beliefs, and goals. Erikson saw the young adult mind as one in a "moratorium" between the morality learned in childhood and the ethics to be developed by the adult. The young adult has to learn the roles that they will have as an adult. Erikson believed that the focus is on two kinds of identities: sexual and occupational.

Young people determine who and what they want to be with regard to their future occupational identity. They also are concerned about their body image as it concerns their sexual identity. When they come to terms with these concerns they have reached what Erikson calls *Fidelity*. This *Fidelity* involves being able to commit one's self to others on the basis of accepting others, even when there may be ideological differences.

A failure to establish a sense of identity within society (I don't know what I want to be when I grow up) can lead to role confusion. This role confusion involves the individual not being sure about themselves or their place in society. Here we see that pressuring someone into an identity can result in rebellion in the form of establishing a negative identity, and in addition to this feeling of unhappiness arises that makes things unsettling for the young adult.

Erikson helped us see young adulthood as an active and significant time of personal growth. However, he is vague about the causes of development. What kinds of experiences do people have to resolve the psychosocial conflicts and move from one stage to another are unclear? There is no universal mechanism to resolve a crisis in his theory. His theory does not explain how moving from one stage to another influences personality which is the primary manifestation of one's identity. However, one's personality is developing throughout a lifetime and describes the characteristics of patterns of thoughts, feelings, and behaviors that make a person unique and makes them who they are.

Personality can change as conflicts are resolved, but usually they remain stable over a lifetime. Generally, personality is organized and consistent. Although it is generally stable, the environment and individuals in the environment can influence it. Personality can cause certain behaviors to happen. We address this concept of personality change later in the section on self-perception.

Stage 6 makes some contributions here by helping us to understand how the individual relates to others in their world, or the new environment they enter. It moves the young adult to establish either intimate relationships with others or find themselves in a state of isolation.

Erikson's contribution is to explain changes over a lifespan by looking at social interaction and relationships in the development of an individual and their growth. In his view, Erikson says that social interaction is constantly changing due to the new experiences and the information that we acquire in our daily interactions with others throughout life. In young adulthood, outside forces coming from the family and peers play a role in developing who one is becoming.

Nicolon (2000) and more contemporary psychologists support the views of Erikson and Havighurst. Nicolon states, "Young adults attempt to develop identity and ideas about strengths, weaknesses, goals, occupations, sexual identity and gender roles. Teens 'try on' different identities, going through an identity crisis, and use their friends to reflect back to them" (bullet point 5).

Boeree (2006) thinks that "if you successfully negotiate this stage, you will have the virtue Erikson called Fidelity. Fidelity means loyalty, the ability to live by societies standards despite their imperfections, incompleteness and inconsistencies. Fidelity means that you have found a place in that community, a place that will allow you to contribute" (stage five, paragraph six).

Marcia: Identity States

Marcia (1980), like Havighurst and Erikson, sees this focus on identity development as crucial to young adulthood. Marcia proposes four Identity States. He focuses on ideological and occupational aspects as the underlying constructs that define the young adult. He sees young adults moving through a decision-making process that shifts from parental chosen to individual self-chosen positions ideologically and occupationally. He does not have the same concern with sexually or physically based aspects of growth. His work focuses on Identity States as described here.

According to James Marcia identity development is, "An internal, self-constructed, dynamic organization of drives, abilities, beliefs, and individual history. The better developed this structure is the more aware individuals appear to be of their own uniqueness and similarity to others and of their own strengths and weaknesses in making their way in the world. The less developed this structure is, the more confused individuals seem about their own distinctiveness from others and the more they have to rely on external sources to evaluate themselves" (1980, p. 5). The identity structure is dynamic, not static. Elements are continually being added and discarded. Over a period of time, the entire gestalt may shift (1980).

Expanding upon Erikson's theory, Marcia developed four Identity States experienced by young adults. They are described here.

Identity Foreclosure

Persons who are also committed to occupational and ideological positions, but these have been parentally chosen rather than self-chosen. They show little or no evidence of "crisis."

Identity Moratorium

Individuals who are currently struggling with occupational and/or ideological issues: they are in an identity crisis.

Diffusion

Young people who have not set occupational or ideological direction, regardless of whether or not they may have experienced a decision-making period.

Identity Achievement

Individuals who have experienced a decision-making period and are pursuing self-chosen occupation and ideological goals.

Understanding these constructs from a psychological perspective is crucial as all of these varied points inform this aspect of human development of growth and the attainment of one's identity.

In the case of each of the three psychologists, we see this focus on identity development in some fashion. This focus relates well to our earlier identification of themes that can drive the selection and instruction of young adult literature. At the heart of the themes and thinking is the young adults' struggle with conflicts, both internal and external. It is these conflicts that help young adults define themselves and change as they grow. We do see a widening circle of influence, as we look at each of the psychologists from physical self to family and peers to external forces and encounters. These shifts can cause internal forces and struggles that must be resolved for maturity to emerge.

INTERNAL CONFLICT AND STRUGGLES AND THEIR IMPACT ON IDENTITY AND GROWTH

The question that drives young adult growth is "Who am I becoming?" This question also may drive us through life, but the major conflicts may come in young adulthood because of a lack of experience to maintain stability and confidence to move forward. This is part of our focus for establishing instruction that is appropriate for young adults.

Who Am I Becoming?

It seems that as young adults face life's issues, and struggle with them, they face and resolve the conflicts that arise. New roles are accepted. Specific problems young adults perceive that they face are addressed with the goal of clarifying oneself. The themes that emerge in their lives often parallel the four themes that we identified earlier.

How Does Conflict Contribute to Identity Development?

Our concern with identity formation in young adults comes from the degree of conflict about many aspects of oneself at that stage of development. The thinking is that young adults begin to recognize who they are and become mature in their thinking and emotional states through the resolution of conflicts. The resolution of the conflict heightens the clarity of identity. These times of conflict may help us see the triggers for transformation, and in turn help us guide young adults in their reading of literature.

Do New Roles in Life Influence Identity Development and Facets of Instruction?

As one assumes new roles, one's sense of identity, level of maturity, and willingness to accept responsibility changes and makes for stronger young adults. Perhaps types of excessive trauma can influence a person's understanding of ideas. Understanding this should help to organize instruction and expectations with regard to reading literature and young adult literature.

These tasks and stages may be the indicators for growth that can guide us in teaching appropriate literature to young adults.

Are There Indicators of Growth?

It is important to see what the indicators of growth may be during this time too. As well as how they influence a young adult's ability to grasp the themes and the issues of literature. At least three indicators merit attention here. They are as follows:

1. *Acceptance of one's place in society*
2. *Acceptance of one's responsibilities*
3. *Acceptance of one's significance*

As the young adult comes to terms with these three states of acceptance, we see the young adult start to mature. Identity and growth as they are linked to maturity is central to this part of the chapter. We need to characterize this growth in relationship to reading literature. These indicators of growth suggest a greater focus on how the individual recognizes their place in society.

Maturity as a Goal: Becoming a Person and Defining Oneself

Young adults become a person with a clear characterization that defines them as a person who now has assumed different roles and views reflecting their value structure. The three indicators identified here may be clear signs of reaching the maturity that support the type of reading of literature that Rosenblatt puts forth.

The Impact on Reading Young Adult Literature

This psychological development underlies much of the identity change that comes with each new role in life. It is important for us to consider how a psychological framework contextualizes instructional goals, emotional concerns, and responses. We believe that these are the psychological concerns that can and should drive instruction, and that it is important to acknowledge the psychological development of the young adult reader as it influences the reading of a piece of literature. This is because in many ways a text mirrors life experience and life experience frames the many developmental stages of life and growth of individuals as those individuals fit into society or tackle the tasks of life, particularly with regard to establishing one's own identity. Each of these life developments adds a new dimension to the young adult readers' background. These changes may explain why a book read at ten has a new meaning when read at twenty-five.

With the conceptual frameworks of these psychologists in mind, we hope that you can apply your understanding of them to how they influence the instructional goals in teaching young adult literature. We hope that you will consider how both emotional and intellectual concerns influence the understanding of a text and one's response to it, and in turn guide the teacher in developing the student's ability to find meaning in literature.

This understanding of a psychological perspective on adolescent development can be coupled with a sociological perspective that adds a view of development that represents not only the individual's development but also the societal influences on that individual's development. We are hoping that the young adults' recognize that although reading at first is a solitary act that it may also become a means for social exchange of the ideas in a text. So here we move to a look at sociological theory to accomplish this goal.

SOCIOLOGICAL PERSPECTIVES

Group Affiliation, Peer and Environmental Pressure, Self-Perception, and Sociological Support Systems

Group affiliation; peer, environmental, and emotional pressure; self-perception; and sociological support systems contribute to our understanding of how sociological perspectives on young adult identity development may influence reading young adult literature. We consider these factors because they extend the psychological perspective presented in the previous section of the chapter. They also are the core of the discussion because both individuals and groups develop as a result of social interaction.

What Is the Influence of Group Affiliation and Peer and Environmental Pressure? Key Contributors

Sociologists have studied group affiliation; peer, environmental, and emotional pressure; self-perception; and sociological support systems in various ways over time. Several theorists are of interest to our discussion. The individuals that we consider are G. Stanley Hall (2006), Bronfenbrenner (1912, 2000), Larsen (2018), and Lashbrook (2018) because each of them has brought different views to our attention. The ideas of these individuals move us through time bringing to bear the context of the world that they live in.

Hall gives us an early historical perspective; Bronfenbrenner gives us an ecological model on environmental pressure; Larsen gives us a look at good and bad peer pressure and influences; and, finally, Lashbrook gives us a look at emotional dimensions of peer pressure.

An Early Historical Perspective: G. Stanley Hall

During the early 1900s Hall's work began to enter the psychological and sociological thinking of the time. His concept of young adolescence, or as we are calling it young adulthood, as a transitional period in human experience was characterized as subversive or rebellious behavior and biological maturation (puberty) during the ages of fourteen to twenty-four. This age range has varied over time. More contemporary notions based on altered social and cultural norms and biological understandings place the ages at ten to eighteen. We think that the range is eleven to twenty-one.

We begin with Hall because we believe that he has had a major impact on sociological thinking. Hall's focus on males is both interesting and disconcerting, but reflective of his times when males dominated our cultures. It echoes Havighurst's psychological view. It may still hold true for males today even with strong women and minorities' movements surfacing now. His work gives us an historical sense of the early look at young adult development.

Hall's work focused primarily on males, and that their body energy needed to be controlled and channeled. He advocated more sports as opposed to academic study. He pushed for education to foster emotions of patriotism and service. He held obedience and discipline in high esteem, but claimed that these traits were best fostered through supervising physical energy. He said very little about young adult women, as he believed their education should be tailored to their gender role, preparing them for their roles of wife and mother.

This focus on young males tended to see young boys forming specific group affiliations, many focusing on sports- or team-related activities in a variety of environments. It may be the roots of the concept of the "old boys' network" where boys and men developed social or professional goals around those affiliations. His view may contribute to young adult literature by influencing decisions about the need for protagonists' activeness, or the thematic topics of interest. We may see the remains of his views in sports that are highly physical in nature, and that for many still apply primarily to boys.

As time passed, sociologists broadened their views to look at young adults differently. Bronfenbrenner's environmental perspective is a good example of this broadened view and contributes substantially to our work.

An Environmental Perspective: Bronfenbrenner's Ecological Model

Bronfenbrenner (1912, 2006) gave us a look at young adulthood through an environmental perspective rooted in an ecological model. This view is a shift from Hall's by focusing on the environments' influence on how young adults move from a limited environment of family and home to enlarged aspects of the environment that require different interactional skills on the part of the young adult.

Each of his five systems enlarges the young adults' reality and world helping to shape an identity in relationship to the world they inhabit. His model addresses the following questions:

1. How does Bronfenbrenner's ecological model address influences on young adult development?
2. How have the changes in environment influenced young adult development?
3. What kinds of conflicts or deficits does the environmental change create?

A simplified presentation of the model follows (figure 2.2). We took the liberty of taking Bronfenbrenner's categories and arranging them into a nested model that better illustrates the relationship between the systems:

Microsystem: immediate surroundings of family, school, neighborhood, childcare

Mesosystem: between structures such as parent and teacher; church and neighborhood

Exosystem: larger social structure in which the child does not function directly; parent workplace and schedules; community-based family resources

Macrosystem: cultural values, customs, laws, belief systems impact resources

Chronosystem: dimension of time, timing of parents' death, and physiological changes of age

As individuals enter each system we see the individual facing environments that enlarge the number and the type of factors that influence that individual. In turn, the individual may change as they encounter the people and the characteristics of these environmental influences. This movement often requires adaptation to each new environment and creates changes in the persona of the young adult as they grow.

We see this model as a useful guide to how reading literature can help the young adult reader understand the world beyond their immediate experiences. The influence of the Mesosystem and the Exosystem are strong during young adulthood and daily functioning. However, they represent a very small part of a world context.

We believe that moving from these two systems to Macrosystem and Chronosystem is the juncture in the lifespan that brings many of the conflicts that the young adults face. We believe that reading literature can bridge this gap in this stage of the young adults' life by guiding their understanding of the effect of one's environment.

The model shows how as an individual moves from the influence of the family circle to the larger environment changes occur and different affiliations develop. Although eventually there appears to be a chronological stage progression in this model it may be recursive and interactive in an individual's life with environmental factors operating at different times and with slight variations.

One of the key relationships that develop is how the changing workplace influences the family and the individual. Family seems to take a backseat to the workplace regarding influence and affiliations. One of the environments that force the growth adaptation is the workplace. Here the young adult needs

Theoretical Perspectives on the Literary, Psychological, and Sociological Aspects 61

The model in its simplest form has several systems that influence child and adolescent development. They are as follows:

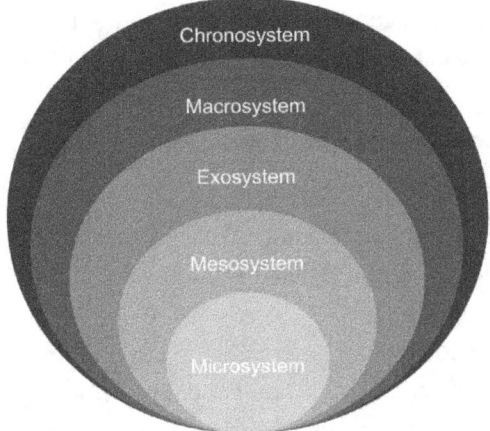

Figure 2.2. Bronfenbrenner's Ecological Model of Young Adulthood.

to adapt to the expectations of others in many ways. The workplace becomes a primary influential environment.

Sometimes a deficit in relationships emerges when young adults move into the workplace. When there is a deficit in emerging relationships there is a declaration of deficiency and a need to obtain help and the deficiency tends to be disruptive. This new instability and unpredictability of family life that may be caused by the expectations of the workplace may be destructive because it changes the mutual interaction with important adults who influence development. As a result, the young adult can develop antisocial behavior where there is a lack of self-discipline and an inability to provide self-direction. Schools and teachers who normally provide stable, long-term relationships and caring relationships that balance the antisocial behavior begin to have less of an influence on the young adult. One of the primary goals at this stage of development is to reduce conflict not only between peers and family but also with the workplace and family life so that learning and good interactions are enhanced.

While Bronfenbrenner gives us a broadened look at young adult development in relationship to environment, and specifically the effect of the workplace, both Larsen and Lashbrook zero in on peer influence, albeit in different ways. Larsen shifts our perception again by focusing on peer influences—a very strong factor in shaping who the young adult is becoming. Again, the individual is shifting away from parental chosen to an individual chosen sense of self, and often influenced by peer associations. Larsen focuses more specifically on exploring good and bad peer pressure. His focus fits into Bronfenbrenner's ecological model in the Mesosystem and Exosystem stages.

The Role of Good and Bad Peer Pressure: Larsen

Larsen (2018) defines peer influence and explains how it works partially as it relates to children and young adults. He sees peer pressure as an influence that is either explicit or implicit: that it is highly visible and initiates behavior, or more subtle in its influence.

Young people become more susceptible to the thinking of others in different ways. This influence begins when children start to pay attention to what others think of them. This influence also causes them to behave differently when peers exert it as they move into young adulthood.

Susceptibility, or the appearance of susceptibility, may be greater for children who do not have as many friends and have a desire to protect the friendships that they have as a way to protect their status. All of what makes them susceptible to influence is not clear. Relationships form among peers in different ways.

Without overgeneralizing, we do see some patterns where girls often form dyads and boys often form groups. Girls often are focused on getting along with particular individuals. Boys often are focused on approval of larger group, or are willing to raise contrary questions. The young adults' ability to recognize the influence of these relationships is part of their reaching maturity. Adults need to help children understand that these attempts to influence are everywhere: to develop an understanding of these influences by peers or by anyone.

Larsen does not limit his concern to peer influence. He holds that the relationship with the parent is important in shaping and supporting young adult development. He contends that we need to understand the characteristics of all influential people to understand how this shaping takes place and follows people across their whole life course. What Larsen doesn't address explicitly is the emotional effects of these affiliations. Here we turn to Lashbrook.

An Emotional Dimension of Peer Pressure: Lashbrook

Lashbrook (2018) adds a slightly different perspective to peer pressure by saying that the emotional dimension of peer pressure has not been addressed adequately. He claims that three issues are absent from dominant models of peer influence. They are as follows:

1. *Neglect of the affective dimension of a young adult's experience*
2. *Tendency to ascribe a passive role to the youth*
3. *A motivational component remains unspecified*

From his view, these three issues translate into three ideas that are significant in suggesting how group influence and interactions work. They are shame, conformity, and isolation. Reitzinger (1995) posits that shame-related feelings may be instrumental in motivating individuals to conform and that peer pressure often produces that conformity. We need to understand the mechanics behind this type of peer conformity.

These shame and conformity stages shape the social bonds that develop from the need to belong. For young adults belonging helps define them in some way. Shame does this by creating a level of social discomfort and embarrassment. We see it manifest itself in several ways (Reitzinger, 1995):

1. *Directed isolation*
2. *Abandoned, separate, isolated*
3. *Ridicule*
4. *Inadequacy*
5. *Discomfort*
6. *Confused/indifferent*

From this view, isolation causes ridicule and a sense of inadequacy. This sense of inadequacy reduces the young adults' ability to address problems with confidence in their choices.

When some sense of belonging or bonding doesn't occur, isolation emerges and becomes a dominant theme. Often we see this with the young adult who doesn't fit anywhere. This state of affairs is difficult for the young adult to navigate.

The Influence of Peer Culture and a Change of Mindset

From this thinking we can understand the influence of the peer culture on individuals, particularly where there is problem behavior. According to Bateman and Currie (2003), a peer culture follows three principles.

1. *Social rules, behavior routine, and negotiation between children begins*
2. *Sharing mutual understanding of actions and norms for procedures enabling systematic interpretation of novel situations*
3. *Engaging in articulation that focuses on themes that are repeated and recognized*

With this peer influence, Brown (1989) believes that multiple cultures emerge with young adults. At least two kinds of groups form—cliques and crowds. The cliques are small, interactive groups, and the crowds are larger groups with more of an emphasis on reputation. Peer acceptance and membership in a clique are seen as important aspects of becoming an adult. In young adulthood some of the impetus for joining a clique may come from the wish to establish an autonomous identity separate from ones' parents to reduce psychological dependency.

Cornell and Murrie (2012) point to the need for friendship and belonging to a community that shares their values, educational goals, and learning needs and provides a safe and personal environment where young adults can learn. Where there is a high sense of community there is higher academic self-esteem, learning orientation, a greater interest in complex problem-solving, development of social skills, and pro-social behavior. There also is a shift in mindset developing.

A primary idea that drives development in this shift in mindset of the young adult is a focus on critical thinking, scientific methodology, and personal awareness. Although this is a substantial shift from earlier approaches, it foreshadows a budding sense of maturity that we hope emerges from adolescent development.

As part of the shift we hope to see a willingness to communicate in open dialogue, use intellectual debate, apply interpersonal reflection, and uncover stereotypes and adolescent biases. These are signs of growth and change over time. This shift is crucial in the sociological view. When and how does the shift happen? Perhaps the young person's self-perception comes into play and has a greater influence on behavior.

The Influence of Self-Perception

In addition to the two concerns of group affiliation, peer influence, and environmental pressure, we need to understand how a person sees the self as this determines with whom they will be affiliated. This personal evaluation of self influences one's own behavior, attitudes, character traits, and affiliations in establishing goals and relationships.

In his work on implicit theories of peer relationships and self-evaluation about personality change, Rudolph (2010) presents two related views—that of entity theorists and incremental theorists. In the case of entity theorists, personal attributes are fixed characteristics that focus on performance-oriented goals and an evaluation of self-negativity in the face of peer disapproval. In the case of incremental theorists, personal attributes are malleable and changeable with goals that shift from strictly performance to incremental growth. The goals are mastery-oriented and focus on learning and developing competence. In contrast to entity theory, where one is liked or disliked, young adults can improve their relationship with their peers, thus, a reduction in the possibility of peer victimization. "Why is this significant? Do people change? What prompts the change? How is this related to the transformative stage of young adulthood?"

The Sociological Support Systems

Another idea that emerges in the sociological perspective is the need for support systems that encourage that growth. These support systems provide a safe passage without cocooning young adults from the complex challenges and difficult choices they face. The support systems help them develop internal control, self-paced learning, a critical evaluation of transmitted knowledge, and realistic risk assessment.

To accomplish these goals young adults need culturally relevant models to help them make the shift. In this shift, the young adult evaluates several things that can help in making choices about peer and group affiliation. They are as follows:

1. *How do we decide how people behave?*
2. *How do we interpret their appearances?*
3. *How do we judge their character* and *who do we think that they affiliate with?*

These points help us to understand important ideas relative to group affiliation, peer and environmental pressure, support systems, and self-perception as they relate to adolescent development, all of which are relevant in decisions about the development of identity through young adult literature.

THE INTERRELATIONSHIPS OF LITERARY, PSYCHOLOGICAL, AND SOCIOLOGICAL PERSPECTIVES

All three theoretical perspectives support our view that the young adult is in a stage of transforming their sense of self. During this time young adults face problems that raise conflicts that need to be resolved for growth to occur. Young adults need ways to grapple with these conflicts that are both personal and social. The dialogue that can be generated around the literature that is appropriate for young adults can support this growth process and help young adults understand themselves and the identity that they are developing.

Although young adults sometimes lack the confidence that they need to face their struggles, the self-reflection and shared perspectives stimulated through reading young adult literature can help them resolve the conflicts that they face. The influence of others supports and shapes the transformative nature of developing their personal identity.

Both the psychological and the sociological perspectives support our decision to choose the theme of identity as the thread and the theme for the reading of young adult literature.

SUMMING UP

Chapter 2 laid out the theoretical underpinnings for the remaining chapters in this book by showing how the literary, the psychological, and the sociological literature contributes to our understanding of the significance of understanding factors contributing to identity development. Each of the theorists gives us a slightly different perspective that helps us identify themes that are relevant in the books that we select for young adults. The theoretical framework we presented supports the need for selecting books that address the conflicts and problems that young adults face, and give them a way to understand the issues of life and their stage of life.

Chapter 3

The Role that Questions and Inquiry Play in Nurturing an Understanding of Young Adult Literature

OVERVIEW OF CHAPTER 3

Chapter 3 moves from the theoretical underpinnings of our endeavor to the more practical aspects of teaching young adult literature. Although there are many goals associated with questioning and inquiry strategies, we believe that questions and inquiry strategies can be designed to include the personal exploration of texts, as well as the academic responses to reading those texts.

This chapter poses examples of frameworks and types of questions that support the three perspectives discussed in the previous chapters, namely, the literary, psychological, and sociological perspectives. To accomplish this goal, this chapter considers the works of both Benjamin Bloom and Howard Gardner as frameworks that offer a conceptual understanding of the various levels and dimensions of questions and inquiry.

Once again, we also emphasize the fidelity that the work of Louise Rosenblatt brings to the ideas of the critical importance of personal response and exploration. Her theories are especially applicable when considering the relationship among the three perspectives and the development of young adult identity and growth. Bloom's and Gardner's works add another dimension to guiding this development.

Finally, we integrate what we have said here in relationship to the Continuum of Engagement, Transaction, and Understanding Model presented earlier in this book.

We hope that we are laying some of the foundation for developing specific instructional plans for traditional texts, contemporary ones, and also multi-modal venues.

QUESTIONS GUIDING THE READING

Why do we use questions for discussion and evaluation of readers' understanding of young adult literature?

How do we develop questions and inquiries to evaluate the student's ability to respond to questions?

In what ways does viewing questioning and inquiry through the lenses of literary, psychological, and sociological perspectives have the potential to positively impact students' growth?

In what way does understanding Bloom's Taxonomy help teachers move through the various personal and academic, intellectual levels of thinking?

In what ways does acknowledgment of Gardner's Theory of Multiple Intelligences influence our awareness of our accepted practices of designing questions and evaluation tasks that require a response that focuses on an overall understanding of the text not only through language-based responses but also through additional ways to instruct and to assess the student's kinds of understanding of the message?

In what ways does an understanding of Louise Rosenblatt's Theory of Transactional Reading alter our understanding of the importance of the teacher's initial questions?

In what ways does this discussion relate to the earlier Continuum of Engagement, Transaction, and Understanding Model?

QUESTIONS, INQUIRY, AND IDENTITY

Questions are woven into our lives in fundamental ways. On a practical level, questions help us negotiate each day. Using questions such as "Where did I leave my car keys? What will be the best route to avoid traffic? Who is carpooling to soccer today?" will help us recall important facts that serve to support the structure of our daily lives.

Asking questions also serves not only to help us function in the practical sense but also to reflect more deeply about our lives and the lives of others. Considering questions such as "In what ways does this situation help me develop my strengths? In what ways does my personal life contribute to the person I want to be? In what ways can I ensure that my life impacts society in a positive way?" will lead us to a better understanding both of others and of ourselves.

Additionally, questions serve as a way to help us think about the decisions we make and the choices that we have. Reflecting on questions such as "How will I find the personal strength when confronting overwhelming challenges? How can I begin to understand how I can choose positive responses in dealing with adversity? In what ways can I apply what I have learned from facing adversity? In what ways can I apply what I have earned from facing diversity to the future challenges that I might face?" will ensure that we are forging positive paths to develop a healthy identity within the context of the past, present, and future. These too are crucial questions that young adults face daily in their most transformative years, and may help us to understand how reading young adult literature can help young adults move toward maturity.

Many times, formulating questions is the first step in learning for young adults with regard to life, and also with regard to the reading of various types of books. Encouraging students to grapple with questions that nurture thinking will help them formulate their own substantive questions.

As readers begin to ask and answer questions, it is critical for teachers to ask questions that help students to clarify their thinking rather than limit their perspective. A general question such as "What do you think about the book?" opens a discussion in a way that welcomes and validates a personal response. It also gives the teacher a sense of where the student is functioning with regards to the book, that is, are they embracing or rejecting the book, and why. Subsequent questions such as "Tell me more about the thinking that led you to form your idea?" or "What motivated the character to act in such a cruel manner?" provide students with opportunities to deepen their thinking.

Questions also help us to clarify confusing situations, to explore new areas of interest, and to strengthen our analytical skills. Questions assist us in understanding people, and in learning about the beliefs that support our decisions as well as the decisions of others. The questions that we ask, or learn to ask, are often rooted in our own identity, and are part of our goal for instructing young adults on their own journey.

Good questioning techniques provide students with time to think before requiring a response and also encourage students to appreciate the possibility of the multiple interpretations of literary, psychological, or sociological perspectives, as well as the perspectives of other readers give.

THE RELATIONSHIP TO LITERARY, PSYCHOLOGICAL, AND SOCIOLOGICAL PERSPECTIVES AS RELATED TO PERSONAL AND ACADEMIC READING: CONCEPTS AND CONTRIBUTORS

The previous section has touched upon the relationships of these three perspectives already. In this next section, we hope to make these relationships more explicit for the purpose of addressing both personal and academic concerns. Of primary concern is the belief that the benefit of reading and contemplating young adult literature is that the reading experience supports the process of delving deeply into these dimensions of the young adults' identity and understanding of themselves individually and as part of social interactions by developing their own ability to have good personal and academic, intellectual readings and responses to what they read. All three perspectives come together and influence what the reader takes from the text.

Literary Perspective

The literary perspective helps the reader engage in the text and apply the literary aspects and affective stance needed to process the text as literature that expresses the human condition. This literary perspective changes and deepens as students engage with various levels of text. Certainly, students' past reading experiences prepare them to engage more effectively with higher-level texts. Students who read a great deal during childhood are generally better prepared for the increased level of difficulty of books for young adults. These students are better prepared to engage more easily with the intricacies of plot development, complexity of characters, subtlety of themes, and the sophistication of language as the texts become more challenging. In many ways, students draw from the depth of their literary experiences to ensure meaningful transactions with the text.

This points to the importance of skillful teachers who can match a reader with a text that is not only interesting to the student but also written at a level which allows for the student to engage fully with the text. Similarly, through thoughtful questions or inquiry strategies teachers can encourage students to enhance their literary and academic learning by drawing from their literary reservoirs to further their learning. For example, questions such as "In what ways does this book remind you of any other books you have previously read?" allow students to make comparisons between books that enhance understanding and deepen their literary knowledge. Such questions can be scaffolded to bring students to new knowledge and ideas. The nature and level of engagement influences the kind of transaction for both the individual and their psychological constitution as well as how the individual responds to group perspective, interaction, and dialogue.

Clearly, identifying books that readers find relevant increases the opportunities for growth not only from a literary point of view but also from a psychological and sociological viewpoint. These three perspectives are often intertwined. Readers who identify with characters and events in a book are rewarded by not only seeing themselves in a book but also seeing beyond themselves in the same book. These opportunities for personal growth are embedded not only in a literary and academic perspective but also in the psychological and sociological perspectives.

Psychological Perspective

Although we discussed the psychological perspective in earlier chapters, we return to it now to further illustrate the way in which these three perspectives are often intertwined. The psychological perspective brings to bear the young reader's stage of emotional, social, and cognitive development as the reader is still developing a sense of who they are becoming.

This book is particularly focused on identity and, specifically, identity in relation to young adults. Oftentimes, when describing the process of identity formation, behavior is considered (Havighurst, 1956; Erikson, 1968). In many ways, outward behavior offers us a window into a person's inner being. As young adults grapple with identity, their behavior often reflects their personal struggles. This time of development can be charged with emotion, and young adults can look to literature to find a medium to grapple with their emotions.

The emotional process often becomes evident, particularly when students experience emotional tension regarding the complex behavior of literary characters. Literature provides students with an opportunity to acknowledge, discuss, and respond to an emotionally charged context. Literature further presents students with opportunities to consider alternative behaviors and progress through emotional responses to rational thinking.

Throughout her writings, Rosenblatt stresses that the literature itself and the discussions that follow may later be assimilated into actual behavior. When a teacher incorporates the emotional response to literature into the discussions of literature, there is great potential for learning and action. The classroom environment in which students can exchange ideas and perspectives can contribute greatly to the way a student learns to assimilate ideas into actual behavior.

This capacity and the opportunities for students to envision themselves in a variety of situations and consider the character's actions and the consequences that follow have the potential to directly influence the character formation of young men and women. Teachers can facilitate the process of supporting students in this process of forming their identities with questions such as "Can you identify two or three qualities within the character that you found worthy of admiration?" or "Can you recall two or three qualities with that character that disappointed you?"

Young adults are reading to gain their own perspective and interpretation of the text. It is this level or aspect of the transaction that the reader takes to respond to a group's dialogue on a text. They also are at a time in their lives when they are much influenced by their peers and hopefully the adults who care for them. Understanding these sociological influences brings to bear the final perspective on developing their identity.

Sociological Perspective

The sociological perspective brings to bear how the reader tests and integrates an individual reading and interpretation when tested against the interpretation of a larger group. The reader, when functioning in a group, will have different ways of integrating a group's interpretations of the text ranging from complete agreement to highly conflicting points of view. The group then explores the range of interpretations in an open and reasonable way as possible through dialogue.

Exploring this range of interpretations helps the young adult see how others may look at conflicts, dilemmas, or characters' actions differently. In some instances, the young adult may not have seen the consequences, both positive and negative, of an action or a decision. They may not see the way that harm may come to a character that behaves a particular way.

Within a class discussion of teacher and their students, the response may vary with regard to the stage of maturity of the readers. Peers may see things through less mature eyes than the eyes of an adult. In part, the level of maturity may be attributed to life experience. While the mature response of the teacher may reflect their life experience, similarly the less mature responses of the students may reflect their lack of life experience. In this setting the more mature viewpoint of the adult presents an opportunity for students to broaden their perspective, deepen their thinking, and begin to understand the consequences of their actions.

There may also be, within the classroom discussion, a range of interpretations from peers that reflects a depth of understanding that may be surprising for adolescents. In a similar way that comments from a teacher may foster growth, comments from peers may also place the young adult in a position to consider and choose among various interpretations of a text.

The influence of what they hear can help a young adult reader either confirm or alter their interpretation, and this may result in a transformation of themselves through growth or it may lead to stagnation within a less mature stage of development. The young adult may then choose between the interpretation of the peer group and that of an adult who has had a greater life experience.

Although the power of classroom discussions to assist young adults face the struggles and challenges in their lives is tremendous, we also believe that the power of dialogue and conversation is rooted in compelling topics and materials. Young adult literature provides students with the unique opportunity to engage in discussions about books that reflect the complexity and reality of young peoples' lives.

Recent books for young adults explore topics such as peer pressure, family dynamics, depression, suicide, the environment, economic and racial (in)equality, as well as sexual trauma and LGBTQ+ love. The characters in these stories develop, not in isolation, but within the context of family, friends, school, and society. Not only do these books provide readers with the opportunity to explore these subjects, they also provide young adults with a source of support to assist them as they face complex challenges and difficulty situations.

As these young people negotiate the movement toward adulthood, these books offer a means to help them decide who they want to be, with whom they want to affiliate, how to judge character, and how they can face life's challenges in positive ways. For many young people, these books provide them with the much-needed support to begin to realize that they are not alone but rather that there are in fact many people as well as characters who share their thoughts and beliefs. The readings and discussions can lead them to develop not only a stronger sense of identity but also the capacity to understand that they, too, can contribute to the well-being of our society.

Both groups, peers and mature adults, place the young adult in a position to choose an interpretation of a text. The reader has options to consider about the meaning of the text. The influence of either group can help a young adult reader transform themselves to either grow or remain in a less mature stage of development.

As all three perspectives come together, we find the meaning of the text for the young adult reader. That is, what do they understand? The questioning strategies that teachers use need to draw all three perspectives together in discussion and in instruction.

QUESTIONING STRATEGIES

Questioning strategies can go beyond using direct questions and can take many forms such as personal notebooks, well-developed response guides, and as we move into the digital age, electronic modes of communication. Students also benefit by sharing effective reading strategies, participating in literature circles, or presenting book talks. All of these forms of inquiry encourage students to delve deeper into books and enhance their understanding of themselves, others, their relationships with others, and the world.

Questions and inquiry strategies, both oral and written, have the potential to assist students in delving into texts. When students engage in exploring ideas in writing, they not only are expressing their own ideas but may also be discovering new ideas. Smith (1982) explains, "Writing separates our ideas from ourselves in a way that is easiest for us to examine, explore and develop them" (p. 15).

Again, the goal with these strategies is to help students develop both the personal and academic skills to address some of the elements of the four themes that we identified in an earlier chapter, given our belief that these themes are of relevance to the young adult reader as well as universal in human development and life in general.

BLOOM, GARDNER, AND ROSENBLATT—
MULTIPLE VIEWPOINTS

The substance of the strategies can be guided by the thinking of three individuals—Benjamin Bloom, Howard Gardner, and Louise Rosenblatt. We have given much attention to Rosenblatt in earlier chapters because she holds the literary perspective that we feel is most relevant and useful to our goals in teaching young adult literature. We will return to her perspective later. Here we move to Bloom and Gardner to extend and give guidance for addressing two different lenses to think about and guide instruction relative to questions, inquiry, identity, and evaluation.

Bloom's Taxonomy

Benjamin Bloom created Bloom's Taxonomy in 1956. The original taxonomy focused on cognitive skills associated with knowledge and comprehension through a hierarchical, sequential model of thinking. Since then, revisions have occurred to include skills or processes such as creation (see figure 3.1).

The model remains somewhat hierarchical in structure by focusing on the lower levels of remembering, recalling, and defining. His middle levels focus on applying and analyzing. At the highest level, the focus is on creative, innovative thinking. The actual nature and substance of the questions that are developed as one moves up the hierarchy can allow for both the personal and academic, intellectual reading and response; however, the tendency has been to focus on the academic, intellectual reading.

This structure of Bloom's Taxonomy is a bit different from Rosenblatt and Gardner in this regard; however, its application or implementation can allow for some recursive movement among questions from different levels. This recursiveness along with some structure is what we aim for here.

Teachers often like the structured progression of questions implicit in Bloom's model because they feel it is a logical progression through one's thinking. This may be the case; however, reading literature through Rosenblatt's lens suggests that a different process may be in play. It may be that a combination of the two views helps us move to our larger goals as stated earlier here. The taxonomy gives teachers a convenient way to frame questions by asking questions such as "How would you identify_____?" or "What do you remember about____?" with the focus at the most basic level of Bloom's Taxonomy. The danger is leaving the reader at that level of thinking just because it is so easily measured and less open to interpretation.

Questions at subsequent levels such as "What biases might exist in the story?" focus on higher levels of analysis and evaluation. And questions such as "Can you create a haiku about the rain forest?" focus a bit more on creation. Unfortunately, we don't always get to the higher levels of the taxonomy in classroom discussions because they may lead to uncomfortable conflicting views of teachers and students, or among students. They also lead to less controllable and more time-consuming dialogue exploring ideas not predicted by the teacher.

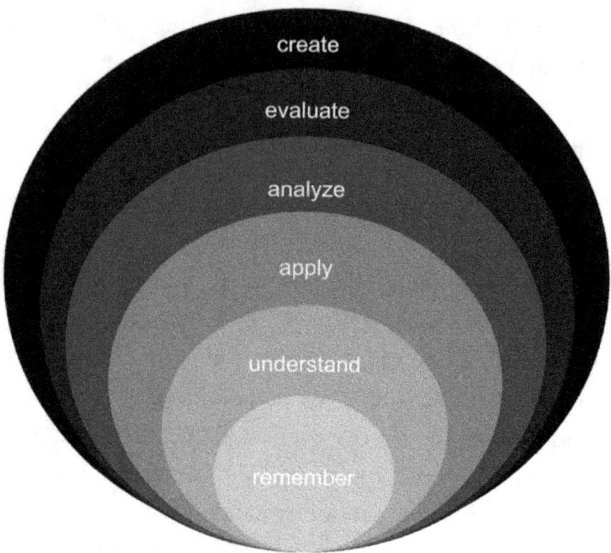

Figure 3.1. Bloom's Revised Taxonomy.

As a reminder of the taxonomy we have provided a visual of it to illustrate the levels outlined by Bloom (figure 3.1). This model is a revision of the hierarchal model often used to represent Bloom's Taxonomy, adapted by the Professional Development Team and the Online Learning team at the University of Sheffield. We feel this nested model better represents the relationships between each level.

This is not to say that Bloom's Taxonomy is not helpful or useful. We have included it here because we think it is the one most often followed in much classroom instruction and materials. The taxonomy can provide a baseline for classroom practices. However, we think that it has limitations that can be addressed by considering other lenses such as Howard Gardner's Theory of Multiple Intelligences and Rosenblatt's perspectives.

Gardner's Multiple Intelligences

Moving beyond Bloom's Taxonomy, Dr. Howard Gardner's Theory of Multiple Intelligences also provides a lens through which to view questioning and inquiry. This theory was developed in 1983 by Howard Gardner of Harvard University, and still maintains its place in the educational world.

The theory suggests that the traditional view of intelligence, determined by calculating an IQ score, is limited. Gardner proposed eight different types of intelligences that present a broader view of intelligence than previously held views. It also extends Bloom's view as represented in its taxonomy. The eight intelligences are as follows:

1. Linguistic intelligence
2. Logical-mathematical intelligence
3. Spatial intelligence
4. Bodily kinesthetic intelligence
5. Musical intelligence
6. Interpersonal intelligence
7. Intrapersonal intelligence
8. Naturalistic intelligence

Where this view may have relevance to our goals in this book is related to the kinds of questions, strategies, and activities that a teacher uses in the teaching of literature that tap a variety of dimensions of students' abilities, or in this case, intelligences that differ from Bloom.

We believe that the Theory of Multiple Intelligences may transform the way teachers present material, design instruction, and design inquiry strategies and questions to students. Gardner's theory suggests that teachers frame lessons and inquiry strategies so that students have a variety of ways to respond to their reading that uses not only traditional language-based questions but also music, art, reflection, and more approaches that can help with evaluation of readers' responses to what they read.

Broadening the perspective on intelligence for all students may help some students who are accustomed to only one avenue of expression to develop other ways also. For example, images within a novel may evoke a deep response. Encouraging students to present the image through painting or sculpting may serve as a way to assist students in deepening their understanding of that particular scene or image. Similarly, many students are affected by music and when students create songs, raps, or original musical scores to explain concepts or themes, they are actually seeing and sensing the literary work in a creative and meaningful way.

Having multiple ways to experience a literary work such as acting it out, discussing it, creating visual representations, using music to capture varying moods or events in the literary work serves not only to assist all students in participating in the experience but also to deepen and enhance the experience of the reading experience for all. This is not to say that these avenues of expression serve only as ends in themselves but rather as a means for all students to view the literary work in more expansive ways.

Skillful teachers can help students view these interpretations in many ways. For example, the student responses can be part of the entry point of personal response, the engagement aspect of reading, or the more detailed literary discussion of the form of the literary work. Additionally, the student responses may be viewed through the lens of identity.

We believe that incorporating Gardner's Theory of Multiple Intelligences serves to nurture the experiential nature of reading. Each of these alternative modes of response can add to the reader's deepened understanding of the text.

The challenge is for teachers and administrators to embrace this philosophy so that each child can learn in ways that maximize their potential and growth while shaping their identity (Armstrong, 2000). Students do not have to experience all eight ways of learning with each lesson or activity but rather have to be allowed to explore the different ways to learn over time, so that they can see the possibilities for expressing their understanding of what they read.

A RETURN TO ROSENBLATT'S LENS AND THE FORMATION OF IDENTITIES

We have said that one central benefit of reading literature is that experiencing literature helps us to learn about ourselves, others, and our place in the world. For Louise Rosenblatt, the study of literature should be an exploration. Her words emphasize her belief in the vital importance of experience. She states that literature should be valued "as a means of enlarging the world, because through literature students acquire not so much additional information as additional experience" (Rosenblatt, 1995, p. 38).

Experiences are what help form our identity. Engaging with characters, conflicts, and resolutions assists the reader in forming an identity. A central component of forming an identity is listening to oneself as well as others, and then discerning one's own identity.

Teachers play an important role in encouraging every student to experience literature as a way to impact the development of their unique identities. One way teachers can assist students in engaging with literature to help them form identities is through posing questions that validate the importance of the unique, personal response of each student as the gateway to further development of more advanced and sophisticated readings of a text.

Rosenblatt is emphatic, as are we, that the entry point for students' discussion should begin through questions that support personal response. The following three questions are examples that invite students to consider their personal response to the story, poem, play, or other forms of literature:

What did you think of the story, poem, play, or text?
What meaning did the story, poem, play, or text have for you?
What struck you as meaningful as you read the text?

We believe that student's personal response requires and encourages engagement, something that is crucial for the student to obtain any kind of meaning from the text. Further questions that would begin to probe the students' engagement in the text are as follows:

Was there a point in this piece when you became engaged, and if so, what was it?
What was reading this text like for you? For example, were you living within the book to such an extent that you felt as though you were no longer reading but rather living within the text?
Were there particular words, phrases, or sentences that evoked a strong response within you? If so, please share them, and the effect that they had on you?

These are just a few questions that can help the reader enter the text in a meaningful way to them and help the teacher know what the reader is taking from the reading as well as where to go with further discussion. They are part of the engagement phase of the Continuum of Engagement, Transaction, and Understanding Model presented earlier in the book.

BEYOND THE PERSONAL RESPONSE

While Rosenblatt felt that the personal response was critical, she recognized the need to go beyond this entry point to connect with more academic, intellectual readings of the text. She also saw moving beyond this entry point to connect literary experiences with the broad goals of educating students to live in a humanistic society where both empathy and critical thinking are needed to interact with others as well as to make informed decisions in the society they live in.

Literature provides an invaluable resource for students to learn to become compassionate, engaged, and educated citizens. Critical thinking questions can lead the students in this direction at a time when our world is in desperate need of these kinds of people.

The experiences with literature offer the students a way to connect their life experiences to a text while they simultaneously experience something from the text that may help their own development. The personal reading and nature of fiction in particular allows a reader a glimpse not only into themselves, but also into a world beyond themselves that reflects a host of social concerns, both psychological and sociological in nature. Here is where the reader moves into more academic and intellectual readings of texts that require guidance from the adept classroom teacher.

Examples of questions that foster this development of empathy and critical thinking are as follows:

What conflicts were the characters facing?
What societal factors helped create the conflict?
In what ways does the author present the societal and cultural context of the time?
In dealing with conflict, what motivated the character to make the decisions they made?
Was there a character with whom you empathized? What was it about this character that caused you to feel empathy for them?
Can you identify two or three qualities within the character that you found worthy of admiration?
Can you recall two or three qualities within that character that disappointed you?

These questions tend to focus on character because most readers focus their reading on the people in the text first, and then move to broader concerns either through the character and their actions and decisions, or because the readers are bringing wider perspectives to the meaning of the text. Here the readers move on to address the following types of questions, usually with the teacher's guidance:

Do you hold any perspectives on life that have been validated by the events of the text?
Are there any ways in which your viewpoints on life have been challenged?
Is there something about the way the text is written that helps you to answer these questions better? Is it the language, the structure, or something else?

This last question helps move the reader to more formal concerns with the text, ones that usually are best addressed once the personal responses are recognized. On the Continuum of Engagement, Transaction, and Understanding Model the readers are moving along the first level of reading for meaning where they become engaged in more academic, intellectual readings of the text.

The next section looks at the relationship of what we have been saying to the Continuum of Engagement, Transaction, and Understanding Model (figure 2.1).

THE RELATIONSHIP TO CONTINUUM OF ENGAGEMENT, TRANSACTION, AND UNDERSTANDING MODEL

Instruction that uses the ideas that we have been presenting in this chapter represents and guides the process of reading literature as described in the Continuum of Engagement, Transaction, and Understanding Model presented earlier in this book. Here we will try to illustrate how this is so.

First, the teacher's purpose for an instructional approach to the text can be guided by what we said about engagement and entry into a text. Where both the teacher and the student enter the text with regards to their level of understanding and purpose for reading will direct the kind of transaction that they have with the text. If the purpose of both the teacher and the student is to read to live through the book's portrayal of the life experience without an explicit focus on specific types of analysis, the transaction may be more personal and relaxed than if the reader is engaged in a critical analysis of the text.

The interaction or transaction level of processing the text will influence the response of the reader in terms of their interpretation of the text. Students also can be motivated by the intensity of their engagement. It is this type of engagement that will lead them to a deepened understanding of the text.

Second, where the problems and the themes of the text are relevant to the reader, and conceptually within the reader's experience and skill, either life experience or academic experience, the engagement, transaction, and understanding will vary tremendously.

Often when the message of the text is not explicit, different readers may have a range of interpretations, all valid when explained or substantiated by reasonable inferences drawn from the text. Here we see the reader's background having a bearing on the interpretation. In the case of the young adult reader, they may or may not have the life experience or cognitive or emotional wherewithal to understand what the author is doing to deliver the message. Their understanding of the author's message may not go far on the literal-interpretative level of level three of the model. The nature of the transaction may be very text-based.

Third, the reader's affective and personal state can influence the reading of a text to the point where the reader finds it difficult to even enter the text. For example, the reader who simply doesn't like fantasy will find it difficult to become engaged in a book like *The Hobbit* or the *Harry Potter* series. They are not allowing their imagination to be brought to bear in their reading.

When they love reading fantasy, they find themselves lost in that imaginary world created by the author of the text. How immersed a reader can become in a text makes a great deal of difference in how the reading affects the reader, both emotionally and intellectually.

Fourth, the nature of formal instruction can have an influence on how far the reader goes in reaching an intellectual, formal reading of the text. Certainly a reader who has a literary background that has been cultivated by the classroom teacher will see aspects of a text differently than a reader who has not had an instruction in the literary aspects of a text.

Texts read differently because of a chasm created by not having this instruction to having it. This skill integrated with an appropriate level of cognitive and emotional development enhances the reader's ability to understand more difficult text.

Fifth, the reader's ability to orchestrate the synthesis of the skills needed with each of the three levels is key to a satisfying reading of the text. Without the synthesis, the reading may be limited and the reader's understanding of the message is incomplete. The answer to the question "Where does meaning reside?" may be quite constrained.

Our hope is that the Continuum of Engagement, Transaction, and Understanding Model represents how these aspects of reading literature lead to a deepened understanding of the text.

SUMMING UP

The importance in having a range of lenses for questioning and inquiry has been emphasized here because we believe that it enriches the experience of reading young adult literature. The range of questions and modes for inquiry is a mechanism for developing the synthesis of the levels of the Continuum of Engagement, Transaction, and Understanding Model. This, in turn, helps the reader see where meaning resides, and also in what ways this reading becomes meaningful.

Chapter 4

Media, Technology, and Literature

OVERVIEW OF CHAPTER 4

Media have always played an influential role in the dissemination and teaching of literature. At its most basic definition, media are tools for communication purposes, and various mediums have been around for centuries or more (think books, newspapers, etc.). Technology is yet another tool that allows us to communicate, and it is not always digital although we often conflate the two given the inundation of digital tech in this age. In fact, the mechanical printing press is a form of technology, one that allowed the reproduction of books to increase to a point where they became a mass medium and democratized access to information.

Media and technology put books into our classrooms, and as new types of media and technologies have emerged, they have changed the way we teach literature. Learning about, analyzing, and commenting on literature is no longer relegated to books, term papers, and text. It has expanded to include many types of media, such as video, audio, and web-based tools. This chapter will explore this evolution and touch upon some of the ways media, technology, and literature interact in this digital age.

QUESTIONS GUIDING THE READING

How has technology redefined what it means to be literate?
What should be included in this new definition of literacy?

In what way can Web 2.0 technologies (blogs, wikis, and podcasts) be used in instruction in literature?

What specific skills are needed in order for an individual to effectively use the Internet and other Web 2.0 technologies in teaching literature?

Who benefits from the inclusion of media and technology into the teaching of literature?

THE FUNDAMENTAL CONCEPTS OF TECHNOLOGY AND MEDIA

Technology and Media

Oftentimes, we conflate technology and media. In this age, when often the two are interdependent, it is no surprise that many people use the terms interchangeably. However, there are differences, and it is important to distinguish between the two.

What Is Technology and How Has It Redefined Literacy?

Technology is, at its most basic definition, a tool. When we think of technology in relationship to media, it refers to the tools that are used to create media. Technology is not always digital, and in fact, it has analog roots. For example, as mentioned earlier in this chapter, the mechanical printing press, which was invented during medieval times, allowed for the mass production of books. This completely transformed literacy as a skill only relegated to those from wealth and power.

As access to texts became more commonplace, a literate middle class emerged, changing the face of the economy and eventually leading to a more literate European society. Similarly, this progress was made on other continents as well—as technology improved, literacy followed.

What Is Media and How Has It Redefined Literacy?

As previously stated, media includes books, and with the mass production of books, literacy became widespread. However, these days when we think of media, we often picture video and audio. Multimedia was first conceptualized as a pairing of text with media elements, such as photographs or videos.

As the Internet and its capabilities expanded, multimedia began to include interactive and web-based media. Contemporary media also includes digital media, social media, and animation.

FORMS OF MEDIA AND TECHNOLOGY AND THEIR TRANSFORMATIONS

Radio

Radio is one of the oldest forms of mass media. First invented at the turn of the twentieth century, radio quickly reached around the globe. However, though radio was once the centerpiece of the American family's home, as television became widespread, radio transformed from a source of entertainment to a source of music and news.

Television/Film

Though film predates television, these days the mediums often overlap. Streaming digital media services like Netflix, Hulu, and Amazon are producing films that rival the big Hollywood studios. The dropping price of media production equipment, coupled with the invention of smartphones, and the rise of social media apps and sharing sites such as TikTok and YouTube have allowed people access to these mediums formerly controlled by information gatekeepers.

New Media

Older forms of media were first produced with analog technologies. Radio and television were transmitted through the airwaves, movies were produced using light-sensitive film stock that was hand-edited, and newspapers were printed on a printing press. The invention of computers transformed these mediums into digital media, both in the production and transmission of each.

The invention of the Internet helped further expand digital media into new media by adding an interactive element. New media includes podcasts, wikis, video games, online newspapers, social media, and more. Much like the printing press helped democratize literacy, new media have allowed many communities and social groups who have been silenced to make their voices heard.

Social Media

Social media encompasses anything that allows users to interact with each other via an Internet-enabled device, either in real-time or asynchronous communication. Though today's generation won't remember a time without social media, this form of new media is relatively young. Over the last thirty years, social media has moved from early adopters to the mainstream. According to the Pew Research Center (2019), "In 2005, just 5% of American adults used at least one of these [social media] platforms. By 2011 that share had risen to half of all Americans, and today 72% of the public uses some type of social media."

THE HISTORY OF MEDIA AND TECHNOLOGY IN THE LITERATURE CURRICULUM

Technology and media have always been closely linked to literacy instruction. However, less traditional media took a long time to work its way into the English Language Arts classroom, and more specifically, the teaching of literature of any kind. Though certainly access and ease of use were initial barriers, so was skepticism on behalf of educators. As audiobooks and films became available and popular, many teachers felt that these modalities were shortcuts to the hard work of reading and analyzing literature and did not recognize some of the advantages of these types of materials.

Teachers did not always see how these modalities could enhance the experience with literature by bringing to life much of what was happening in a text. For some students these modalities helped them with visualizing and processing otherwise difficult texts from earlier historical periods or from other cultures. When used well, integrating these modalities into instruction in literature can make a great difference for students' accessing and understanding what they are required to read, particularly when the material does not have an immediate relevance to the students.

However, resistance by teachers did not last, and teachers soon began showing clips from films and incorporating media into the classroom. They began to see, firsthand, how helpful this integration of media was for many students.

Audio recordings, television, films, and computers already have been harnessed as a means to improve and/or augment reading instruction, and more specifically, literature. According to Leu et al. (2004), "Throughout history, literacy and literacy instruction have changed regularly as a result of changing social contexts and the technologies they often prompt" (p. 1574).

In the time line of American reading instruction, technology began to truly influence the curriculum during the period of technological revolution from 1950 to 1965. During this time, technology began expanding rapidly, replacing unskilled laborers with machines. As a result, there was new emphasis on literacy skills in public education as society tried to better prepare its students for the unknown jobs of the future (Smith, 2002). With these basic changes in the types of technology that were developing, schools and teachers started to rethink the way that they taught many subjects, literature included.

TODAY'S STUDENTS AND TECHNOLOGY

Today's twenty-first century students, often referred to as the "Net Generation," are radically different from those at the turn of the twentieth century (Alvermann, 2001). As a society, we have left the age of industry and entered the information age, which is dominated by a fast-paced exchange of knowledge, primarily via new technologies (Edwards, 2010), having significant effects on the students we teach. Many students are interacting with the new technologies outside of the classroom context and may be learning different ways of processing information and text.

Consider these statistics from Pew Research Center's report on Teens, Social Media and Technology 2018:

- 95 percent of teens now report they have a smartphone or access to one.
- 88 percent of teens have a desktop or laptop computer at home.
- 45 percent of teens say they use the Internet "almost constantly."

These digitally immersed, twenty-first century students need to be prepared for a very different global economy than their twenty-first century counterparts (Leu et. al, 2004). No longer is it enough for students to have basic literacy skills; today's students need to be able to understand and communicate in a world of ever-changing technology (Coiro et al., 2008; Leu et al., 2004).

Students Being Served by Incorporating Technology into the Curriculum

Not only are these digitally immersed students being served by our inclusion of media and technology but also there are other students who can be served with these efforts. In general, media and technology can help us with differentiating instruction for all students, particularly those with different learning styles, disabilities, and different academic skill levels. Furthermore, the range of racial, cultural, linguistic, and socioeconomic diversity among America's schoolchildren grows wider each day (Edwards, 2010) and can be addressed with certain kinds of media and technology.

Alvermann (2001) points out, "Effective instruction builds on elements of both formal and informal literacies. It does so by taking into account students' interests and needs while at the same time attending to the challenges of living in an information-based economy during a time when the bar has been raised significantly for literacy achievement" (p. 5).

A diverse student population brings with it a wide range of educational needs that in some way may be served with the use of media and technology. Given the stark disconnect between the needs of today's students and the curriculum designed to teach children of the industrial age, there is a call to revolutionize the curriculum within our public schools. Such change involves major implications for instruction and the language arts, particularly with our concerns with literature.

THE CHANGING FACE OF LITERACY

Yet again, education is at a crossroads where new technologies are changing the face of literacy, prompting a call for the transformation of the language arts and literacy curriculum of America's public schools. Such instruction is often referred to as digital literacy, new literacy, multimodal literacy, or multiliteracies (Coiro, et al., 2008; Smolin and Lawless, 2003). Though the terms may vary, they all refer to proficiency using technology, multimedia, and the Internet.

This evolving concept of literacy also has much to offer teachers of literature should they choose to consider it as we suggest that they do. The use of multimodal literacies has expanded the ways we acquire information and understand concepts. Ever since the days of illustrated books and maps, texts have included visual elements for the purpose of imparting information. The contemporary difference is the ease with which we can combine words, images, sound, color, animation, video, and styles of print in projects so that they are not only part of our lives but also in ways that young adults can express their understanding of the literature that they read. Our students are ready to embrace any use of technology in the teaching of literature when teachers have been convinced of its value.

STUDENTS AND TEACHERS: THE RANGE AND DIFFERENCES IN SKILLS

Instruction both for teachers and for students is especially important because oftentimes today's students possess more informally learned ability using new digital technologies than their teachers have acquired. In their report on multimodal literacy, The National Council of Teachers of English Executive Committee (2008) noted the following:

> In digital forms, students, even very young students are often more literate in the technical aspects of digital production than many of their teachers. Many students are frequently exposed to popular technologies, have the leisure time to experiment with their own production, and develop the social connections that encourage peer teaching and learning, and may have access to more advanced technology than is available at school. The "definitions" of multimodal composing may be written by educators, but they will most likely have first been pioneered by these young people.

Many of today's students already harness the Internet for educational purposes. According to Pew Internet & American Life Project's 2008 report on *Writing, Technology and Teens*, "94% of teens use the internet at least occasionally to do research for school, and nearly half (48%) report doing so once a week or more often" (Lenhart et al., p. iv). This is not surprising, as the nature of the Internet allows for the proliferation of information.

"Readers in electronic environments are able to gain access immediately to a broad range and great depth of information that not 15 years ago would have required long visits to libraries or days of waiting for mailed replies" (National Council of Teachers of English Executive Committee, 2008, bullet point 5). No longer do students need to spend time flipping through the card catalog of the local library as they pursue academic research. Instead, they can search multiple libraries and sources of information from the comfort of their home with the use of keywords and the click of a mouse button.

However, although today's students have grown up entrenched in a digital world and are comfortable sending emails, tweets, and text messages; surfing the web; interacting with online communities; and creating short videos, their prowess with technology does not necessarily translate to the academic realm (Coiro, 2003). More often than not, students need specific instruction about how to apply their skills to academic endeavors. Without such teaching, students may find it difficult to navigate the digital world for academic purposes (Coiro, 2003). This means that teachers need to know how to use the technology as well as how to instruct their students to use it for academic purposes such as with learning about literature.

The sophisticated searching that students need to do requires guidance for several reasons. First, students need to understand how to choose keywords and how to choose search engines that will be most productive for their research needs. Additionally, oftentimes work posted on websites is inaccurate or lacks scholarly grounding (Smolin and Lawless, 2003). Because of this it is more important than ever that students be taught to examine the resources and the articles that they find on the Internet, using critical thinking skills to evaluate the legitimacy of the website and the author(s) (Smolin and Lawless, 2003). The development of these skills in a formal manner is needed for using Internet resources for research related to the teaching of literature of all kinds.

Reading is not the only skill being impacted by digital technology, writing is also deeply affected. The current emphasis on high-stakes testing within American public schools, in which students are expected to churn out formulaic five-paragraph essays, in no way prepares students for our technology-driven, global community which is based on communication and the exchange of good information. This applies to reading literature also as much writing in the schools is part of testing students' understanding of the texts that they read and then need to write about.

Despite this, many teachers are finding themselves teaching to the test, rather than developing a dynamic, literacy curriculum that incorporates strategies that will enhance the teaching of literature and the writing that students do on literature. Such an approach stymies creativity, innovative thinking, and the synthesis of information from multiple sources—all critical skills that can be enhanced through literature instruction and that are needed in today's global community.

THE CHALLENGES TEACHERS AND STUDENTS FACE

Both students and teachers face challenges with using technology in the classroom and for academic work. Teachers, because many of them did not grow up immersed in the technology, or even if they did, it was not with the idea of using it in instruction in literature. Students' learning, for reasons that we have said, has been informal or has not been translated to academic work. As an educational community, we still have to sort out the useful from the not-so-useful technologies and types of media appropriate for our educational objectives. Some of this will come from use and some from research findings.

For one thing, teachers need to be aware of the cognitive challenges posed by Internet environments before we unnecessarily confuse our competent readers or overwhelm our struggling ones (Coiro, 2003, p. 462). As an example, hypertext and interactive features can offer too many choices and too many animations that may distract and disorient otherwise strong readers as well as struggling ones. So, without strong digital literacy skills, even the most proficient readers, students and teachers alike, may get lost among the copious information available on the Internet (Coiro, 2003). As Coiro aptly notes as follows:

> The Internet, particularly, provides new text formats, new purposes for reading, and new ways to interact with information that can confuse and overwhelm people taught to extract meaning from only conventional print. Proficiency in the new literacies of the Internet will become essential to our students' literacy future. (p. 458)

This statement is significant because it underscores the need for teachers to provide students with explicit strategies for using the new technologies. Otherwise, students will be unable to harness the potential benefits of incorporating new technologies into literacy practices. For example, students who are navigating through a website are often presented with multiple hyperlinks that each provides a different set of information.

Unlike in a book, where information is laid out sequentially, a reader interacting with the website faces a host of possibilities. Because of this, teachers must help students understand how websites, new media, and social media applications work, and provide them with the literacy and technical skills needed to analyze the information before them and then make appropriate choices in their online reading. The double challenge for teachers is first to know how to do this task, and second, to know how to instruct their students to do it well.

INFUSING TECHNOLOGY IN USEFUL WAYS

However, there are many ways to infuse current technologies into the literacy curriculum that may work for the specific teaching of literature. Doing so will allow students to strengthen their traditional literacy skills while learning to navigate the digital world. One way to do so is to incorporate Web 2.0 tools into the curriculum. "Web 2.0 is a descriptor loosely used to note the shift online to spaces that are globally coauthored in real-time, spaces that are collaborative, peer-reviewed, updated and revised" (Bannister, 2008. p. 109).

The three most commonly used Web 2.0 tools are podcasts, blogs, and wikis. Banister claims that Web 2.0 tools have the potential to positively affect the K-12 reading classroom and curriculum. With the added benefit of being both sequential and archivable, blogs, wikis, and podcasts not only add a new dimension to reading and writing instruction, and indirectly to teaching related to literature, by nature of the medium, but also provide a portfolio of student work. Such a portfolio can help teachers see the development of student work as well as summative products. In addition to these general applications of technology to the literacy and literature curriculum, we need to consider more specific concerns with merging instruction in literature with media and technology.

MERGING INSTRUCTION IN LITERATURE WITH MEDIA AND TECHNOLOGY

What Are the Goals?

There is a wealth of research that indicates students who find connections between their own lives and those of the characters within a book tend to engage with the text. Furthermore, research indicates that students who make critical connections with literature are better able to look at themselves and their world with an insightful perspective.

In his book, *Why Reading Literature in School Still Matters: Imagination, Interpretation, Insight*, Dennis J. Sumara (2002) argues that human beings develop their identity through relationships, including relationships with literature. When critically engaged with a book, a student has the opportunity to develop a sense of identity, while simultaneously learning about their place within history and culture.

Sumara (2002) argues for the use of a "Commonplace Book" within classroom teaching, noting, "Reading a common literary text can create opportunities to interpret personal and collective experience, and re-reading that text can generate surprising and purposeful insights" (p. 19). However, Sumara notes that it is vital that students engage with the text, using it as an archival site for personal reflection as well as an understanding of the literature. To do so, he insists, "In order for the intertextual commonplace to become generative, practices of annotating, other forms of responding, and re-reading need to be engaged" (p.34). It is not enough for students to merely flip through the pages—they need to write on their books, speak aloud in class, and work to construct meaning from the text.

Though excellent in theory, one of the major roadblocks to implementing a Commonplace Text in a typical classroom is the lack of funds to supply every student with his or her own copy of the book. Without access to their own text, students cannot annotate as they read, thereby diluting the power of the Commonplace Text. Digital technologies can remove this obstacle.

There is the opportunity to sidestep this issue through the use of electronic books, or "E-books." "These books are available in forms ranging from toy-inspired books, CD-ROM storybooks, online texts, and downloadable books and documents. Much like traditional books, the electronic versions embrace print and illustrations but are viewed on desktop computers, laptops, or hand-held reading devices" (Larson, 2009, p. 255).

Because the text in e-books can be highlighted, annotated, crossed out, and marked in much the same way as traditional texts, they serve as a viable alternative to physical forms of books for a Commonplace Text. Even better, these annotations and comments can be shared with both the teacher and classmates. Further, the integration of traditional literature lessons into new technological formats may be more appealing or familiar to today's digital learners, or even to some students with different learning styles or particular reading disabilities.

Web 2.0 technologies not only have the capability of helping students learn new reading comprehension skills (using both print-based and online texts) but also possess the power to deepen students' understanding of book-based texts. In her report on 'Weblogs and Literary Response: Socially Situated

Identities and Hybrid Social Languages in English Class Blogs,' an informal online discussion of American literature enhanced and deepened these students' understandings of and engagement with texts." Kathleen West (2008) explores the use of blogs to deepen her eleventh grade American Literature students' understanding of their print reading assignments.

West's intention was to "add to the small, growing body of empirical research on digital writing in K-12 classrooms by examining (her) class blogging project in terms of the research question, "What is the nature of literary response as communicated via weblog?" (West, 2008, p. 588). In this particular study, West focused on two female students and one male student in her class. She examined their writing in terms of their socially situated identities. In other words, in these small case studies, she was seeking to see if her students' participation, when posting on the blog, differed from their classroom behavior and interactions.

Upon examining this small amount of data, West concluded that the weblog allowed students to participate in literary discussions in ways that they had not been able to do during teacher-led classroom discussions. Furthermore, she found that students, through writing a serious literary analysis, also used causal discourse not normally found within such contexts.

West saw this observation as a hybridization of genres, noting that the students were "using what they (knew) of other discourses to generate new ideas about literature and new ways of communicating their ideas to their peers" (West, 2008, p. 597). Though small in scope, West's study gives us an insightful look at how blogs can be used to extend discourse of literature analysis and deepen students' understanding of the print-based texts that they are reading in the classroom.

There are several tools similar to the examples we have presented here that can facilitate simple changes that integrate technology into instruction in literature. The next section addresses these tools.

WHAT ARE THE TOOLS TO TIE TECHNOLOGY TO LITERATURE INSTRUCTION?

The Internet has been widely available to the public for over twenty years. During the early years of Web 1.0 interactivity was limited, as the Internet was comprised primarily of static web pages. However, since that time, the Internet has expanded dramatically. "Web 2.0 is a descriptor loosely used to note the shift online to spaces that are globally co-authored in real-time, spaces that are collaborative, peer-reviewed, updated and revised" (Banister, 2008, p.109).

As the technology of the World Wide Web has evolved, so have its applications within the classroom. There are several Web 2.0 tools that are embraced within the education community that have applications to instruction in literature.

E-Books

Electronic books exist in many formats, though Amazon's Kindle readers are probably the most well-known delivery method. Generally cheaper than print alternatives, e-books can be accessed via a web browser or e-reader. As mentioned earlier, e-books allow students to annotate and comment on the text. Furthermore, many e-books have the option to listen to the book being read. This is especially helpful for students with specific reading disabilities, such as dyslexia, who often cannot access grade-level texts independently. Many of the latest e-book programs highlight the individual words and sentences as they are read aloud, helping students to recognize unfamiliar words.

Podcasts

Podcasts are Internet-based audio and/or video recordings that are increasingly being used to augment classroom instruction. Anyone with a computer, a microphone, and an Internet connection can create a podcast—the software is free and easy to use. Some podcasts are available in installments, much like the episodes of a television show. Using software such as iTunes, users can subscribe to podcasts. Once subscribed, new episodes of the podcasts are automatically downloaded to the user's computer (Santosa, 2008). Today's educators are beginning to use podcasts to help students develop reading comprehension skills, fluency, and vocabulary—all skills needed for reading literature well.

Blogs

A weblog, or blog, is a web page akin to an online journal. Though usually written by one person, multiple authors can contribute to one blog. It is chronologically arranged, with the most recent entry displayed first. Prior entries are automatically archived, and bloggers can "tag" their posts with keywords that allow for easy retrieval of posts on particular topics (Anderson, 2007).

Like podcasts, users can subscribe to blogs. They are also free to create and are relatively easy to use. Blogs allow readers to comment on the author's posts, providing a means of communication between reader and writer. Many educators are embracing blogs as a means of extending classroom discussion, and/or improving the reading of literature and writing skills of their students.

Wikis

Wikis are web pages that can be edited by a group of people. They are collaborative in nature, and often serve as a source of information. Wikis differ from blogs in that older versions can be retrieved and examined (Anderson, 2007). Moreover, many educators use Wikis to post class information, assignments, and links to additional resources. Like blogs and podcasts, Wikis are free, as well as relatively easy to set up and use. However, as is the case with many Internet-based resources, students need to develop critical thinking skills when using them.

Google Classroom

Many schools have embraced online course management systems, such as Google Classroom. However, what makes this particular platform unique is that it is integrated with other Google products, such as Gmail (email), Google Drive (file storage and content creation, including documents, slideshows, and spreadsheets), Google Meet (video-chat), Google Scholar (research), Blogger (a blogging platform), YouTube (video production and sharing), and more. Students can use these tools when researching and writing about literature, and teachers can use them to disseminate information to their students.

Internet-Based Applications and Tools

There are a number of tools available free to educators and students. Some are useful as stand-alone applications, whereas others are used in conjunction with other programs or tools. Many teachers integrate YouTube videos into their curriculum, and tools like edpuzzle (https://edpuzzle.com) allow them to embed questions and notes into the video, as well as add their own voice-over. You can even upload and annotate a video you recorded. If you are looking to have your students share video responses, Flipgrid (https://info.flipgrid.com) allows them to record a video and then respond to their classmates' videos. NowComment (https://nowcomment.com) allows teachers to choose a public document or upload one that students can then annotate as a class, writing their own comments and responding to classmates' comments, creating a modern-day commonplace book.

One tool that students can use to create, collect, and curate information is webjets (http://webjets.io). It essentially turns anything you add to it into virtual sticky notes or index cards, which you can visually arrange and organize. This is also a great tool for students working on group projects. Padlet (https://padlet.com) offers a similar tool that allows students to post and respond to each other, share images, and more on a virtual corkboard.

Media projects (videos, podcasts, etc.) can be created using tools such as Audacity and GarageBand (record and edit sound), and iMovie and Adobe Spark (video, animation, and graphics). Tools such as Canva (https://www.canva.com) and Piktochart (https://piktochart.com) are excellent for creating graphic designs (posters, character maps, etc.).

For students looking to augment their media projects, they can download free sounds and music from ZapSpalt (https://www.zapsplat.com), or create sketches for graphic novels or comic books using SketchBook (https://sketchbook.com).

Social Media Tools

Social Media encompass a wide variety of tools. While they originated as Internet-based platforms (such as Facebook or Pinterest), many social media tools are offered as stand-alone applications (such as Snapchat, TikTok, and Instagram). Some of these can be accessed through a web browser, while others are only accessible through a smartphone or tablet. In some cases, a particular social media platform is offered in both formats. Twitter is a great way for students to reach out to their favorite authors. If you are concerned about students actually using these platforms for school, you can still create assignments that are related to them, for example, having them create a mock-up Facebook page for their favorite character in a book or a TikTok-style video that explores the theme(s) of a book.

GENERAL TECHNICAL CONSIDERATIONS

Regardless of what new media tools you incorporate into your curriculum, ensuring all students have access to the appropriate technology is a key component of successful integration. Though many social media apps can be accessed through a smartphone, trying to blog or contribute lengthy text to a wiki would prove cumbersome. Ideally, all students should have access to a laptop, chromebook, or desktop computer so as to take full advantage of Web 2.0 tools and new media. If you want students to create podcasts or videos, access to a smartphone can be crucial. These days, smartphones have excellent cameras, and there are many free apps that allow you to edit audio and video.

ANTICIPATING THE FUTURE

There is no question that media and technology will continue to expand and evolve. While some new media and technology will take root, others will fall to the wayside. Ultimately, the focus should be on creating meaningful instruction that harnesses the benefits of a particular medium or tool. Professional development opportunities must include the latest trends in media and technology. With things changing so quickly, it is no longer enough to participate in a workshop and expect the information to remain relevant for years to come

SUMMING UP

These new media technologies are not only changing the way we define literacy but also contributing to the persistence of traditional literacy skills as they relate to instruction in literature. Reading and writing are integral aspects of these mediums. Without traditional literacy skills, it is not possible to take full advantage of these emerging technologies. These new technologies are not only multimodal applications that require digital literacy skill sets but also have the capability of improving traditional literacy skills. In this way, literacy instruction as it can apply to instruction in literature and Web 2.0 technologies have formed a symbiotic relationship.

Our concern in this book is to raise awareness for the need to incorporate digital technologies into teaching and possible use for instruction and assessment when teaching young adult literature. It is presented as another toolset for educators and students to apply to their ventures into reading literature of all types and forms.

Chapter 5

The Conceptual Background and Practical Ideas for the Instructional Goals for the Development of Identity in Young Adult Literature

OVERVIEW OF CHAPTER 5

Chapter 5 addresses instructional concerns through discussion and illustrations of the principles that drive instruction, approaches to instruction, and samples to illustrate these guidelines. Evaluating and selecting books is also addressed. The chapter integrates instruction with the earlier literary, psychological, and sociological conceptual perspectives. Doing this shows how instruction relates to the theme of the development of identity for the young adult as well as in young adult literature.

The goal in illustrating instruction is to show how the IIU can be coupled with mini-lessons using technology to develop themes and literary aspects of literature. The inclusion of student-developed work illustrates how to shift from teacher-centered instruction to a way for students to take responsibility for their learning.

The hope is that the ideas in chapter 5 illustrate and integrate the ideas presented in chapters 1 through 4 in a form that is useful to the classroom teacher.

QUESTIONS GUIDING THE READING

What are the developmental goals that drive instruction? How do these goals shape instruction?

What should we consider when organizing instruction?
What are the general principles guiding instruction?
How can questions, forms of inquiry, and technology shape instruction?
What are relevant approaches to instruction such as the IIU, the mini-lesson, and student-developed work?
What are the arguments for the choices of themes and issues for developing the concept of identity through this instruction?

DEVELOPMENTAL GOALS GUIDING INSTRUCTION

"How do literary, psychological, and sociological developmental perspectives drive instructional goals?" is a key question for us. Clearly, reading does not occur in a vacuum. The lives that we live provide the context in which our reading occurs, and literary, psychological, and sociological perspectives create the lens through which we view our reading.

Formulating instructional goals that acknowledge the impact of these perspectives on the reading experience requires creating opportunities for students to enjoy stories, deepen their understanding of themselves and others, broaden their perspective, foster their self-awareness, and develop their capacity for empathy and compassion.

This approach recognizes not only the skills involved in reading but also the power of literature. There is a recursive process involved in the way in which the literary, psychological, and sociological perspectives impact the reading experience and the way in which the reading experience impacts the literary, psychological, and sociological growth of the reader. This recursiveness allows for the in-depth reflective reading we aim for in instruction.

Other key questions are "What is the parallel development of developing the identity and the growth of young adult readers with the characters, themes, and issues in the books that they read? Does this parallel development shape instruction?" The answers are significant for shaping instruction.

Oftentimes as students experience young adult novels, they see themselves in the characters' struggles, they hear themselves in the characters' voices, and they empathize with the characters' attempts to confront issues and fears that are all too real for many young adults. Themes such as the reality of death, the pain and the sadness of growing up, alienation from others, and grappling with sexual identity invite readers to both explore the specific theme in the unfolding narrative and evaluate the growth and the behavior of the characters.

An interesting phenomenon occurs when readers live through books: they see themselves and simultaneously they see beyond themselves. Students not only identify with the struggles of the characters but also witness positive behaviors that provide alternative and varied ways to respond to life's challenges. Oftentimes, students internalize events with books and that internalization can impact their own quest for identity.

This parallel development lends itself to instruction that invites discussion, encourages multiple interpretations, and focuses on personal response as an entry to discussion. Personal responses can then lead to more focused conversations that delve into the psychological and sociological aspects of identity as well as the exploration of positive models of behavior that lead to growth and maturity. With this understanding in mind, we move to more specific concerns related to organizing instruction.

ORGANIZING INSTRUCTION

What Should We Consider When Organizing Instruction?

General Structural Concerns

When organizing instruction there are a few concerns that should guide a teacher's thoughts. They are (1) evaluating and selecting books; (2) general instructional principles; (3) integrating questions, forms of inquiry, and thinking into instruction; and (4) understanding of specific appropriate approaches to instruction. These concerns are the focus of this section of the chapter.

Evaluating and Selecting Books

When selecting and evaluating books for use with young adults, either for instruction or for independent reading, we need to consider five categories of concerns. They are as follows:

1. *The reader*
2. *The content of the text*
3. *Instructional concerns*

4. *Staying power*
5. *Appeal concerns*

Within these five categories there are twelve subcategories. They are as follows: *engagement concerns*; *student wants and needs*; *issues, themes, and structure*; *quality and nature of writing*; *challenge level*; *intellectual concerns*; *significance*; *timelessness*; *historical impact*; *teacher concerns*; *curriculum concerns*; and *young adults and adults*.

This section of the chapter characterizes all five of these concerns to help us understand how to select and evaluate young adult books. These categories reflect some of the twelve characteristics identified in chapter 1, but in a slightly different way. The following chart (figure 5.1) summarizes this information.

Integrating Questions, Forms of Inquiry, and Technology into Instruction

Instruction needs to help readers raise their own questions as well as use good teacher-developed questions to guide the reader's thinking about the text. Questions should be varied to prompt different levels of thinking. They should be tied to the development of the themes of the book. Other forms of inquiry, such as a series of statements or problems, should contribute to the reader's ability to reflect upon and apply the ideas in the text to their own lives and experiences. They should lead the reader to a broadened view of the world. Any form of technology should support or enhance the learning experience for the reader. It can be a separate lesson about the technology, but also should be integrated with the books being read.

The Rationale and the Structure for Approaches to Instruction

We selected the IIU, mini-lesson and student-developed work to organize instruction because they give a conceptual, focused approach to instruction. They guide the student from teacher-directed to student-directed reading and thinking in a reasonable, manageable way. They are flexible and comprehensive while still being focused on key instructional goals. They are supportive of learning without being intrusive to the reading and the engagement of the literature. And finally, the goal for each approach is to enhance the emotional and intellectual experience of reading the literature as a means to developing the maturing identity of young adults.

The Conceptual Background and Practical Ideas for the Instructional Goals 103

Category	Description
The Reader	**Engagement Concerns:** • Excitement, interest, engaging, fun, interactivity with text, enjoyment • Develop love of literature • Lead to additional books by author • Impact on the reader • Currency of literature, new books, use of current booklists and resources
	Student Wants and Needs: • What do students want and need, student choices, know your students, who are they, scope of interests, growth, sophistication, age appropriate, range of ability, perspective of Young Adult, predict how students will respond • Relate to protagonists problems and challenges, age of protagonists, credibility of characters relatable characters, identifiable characters, match with self • Point of view is appropriate and understandable • Sense of Optimism, desired accomplishments
The Content of the Text	**Issues, Themes and Structure:** • Issues the readers are facing, multiple issues, type of book (multicultural, fiction, themes with difficult issues,) mirror life stages, perspective of YA, general cultural and world awareness, positive and negative portrayal of characters • Variety of genres, represents genre reasonably well, incorporate many archetypes • Language and structure of the text • Setting is essential, plot development, rich character development, thematic concerns • Visuals are clear and bibliographies are comprehensive
	Quality and Nature of Writing: • Writing quality in general, authenticity of story, elevate literary concepts, plot, pace, literary concepts must be identified and recognizable, deal with literature conceptually, appropriate literary devices, complexity, cohesive plot, common archetypes • Accurate and current information • Ratings by students and others • Teach students about elements of writing and aspects of literature
	Challenge Level: • Balance between challenge and ease, keep expectations high, level of performance, expected education vs fun, appropriate reading level, readability, length, encourage close reading
	Intellectual Concerns: • Invokes higher level critical thinking, depth of thought, expands vocabulary, outside comfort level, engage the imagination, generate broader awareness, world views, catalyst for quality discussions, develop insight, elevate literary concepts
Staying Power	**Significance:** • Does it deal with important concerns and issues beyond immediate interests, extend reader's life experiences, significance of themes, universal themes
	Timelessness: • Young Adult versus Classics, pairing of books, relevant message, impact, significance of message
	Historical Impact: • History of YAL and trends that hold, current events, classic and contemporary, development of YAL literature, cultural and social authenticity of text over historical periods
Instructional Concerns	**Teacher Concerns:** • Experiential and Conceptual level range between teacher and student • Teacher's knowledge of dramatic techniques, teacher needs to read first, teacher's comfortable level with teaching the book, teacher's interest level, enthusiasm of teacher, liking the book, teacher's comfort level with books topic • Balance between ease and challenge, length, encourages student interaction
	Curriculum Concerns: • Applicable to wider curriculum, conditions under which books will be read, purpose and use, educational goals, incorporate themes with other texts
Appeal Concerns	**Young Adults and Adults:** • Build gap between parents and YA • Reaction of parents and administration • Stepping stone to adult difficulty • Check with others who have used the book • Resources for selecting and evaluating books like VOYA • Book clubs • Other external resources

Figure 5.1. Categories and Descriptions for Selecting and Evaluating Young Adult Books.

DESCRIPTION OF THE APPROACHES

IIU—The Model: Description, Value, and Use

The IIU is a flexible model for organizing instruction for units or for briefer multiple day lessons. It allows a great deal of latitude as to the particular focus and the activities that teachers wish to incorporate into their instruction. A number of writers have used the basic structure of the IIU; however, we have enhanced it to give it a better way to organize instruction. What follows is both a visual and verbal illustration of the IIU, illustrations of the IIU, and a description of the process for developing the IIU.

Our work extends many of some previous discussions of the use of *pre-reading*, *during reading*, and *after reading* strategies for instruction by tying together ways to synthesize instruction across all three stages of guidance for reading literature of all genres. The next section of chapter 5 illustrates and describes the IIU and discusses its use and the rationale for its use.

The following visual (figure 5.2) is a depiction of the IIU:

The IIU consists of three primary components of *pre-reading*, *during reading*, and *after reading*, each with its own general goals. In the case of *pre-reading* the goals are to build background and to give a focus for the reading. In the case of *during reading*, it is to guide the reader to various aspects of the book that develop character or theme. And the *after reading* component is to bring the books and ideas together in a synthesis, and then extend the work to other activities and readings.

The model is intended as a flexible model that gives some structure while at the same time leaving adequate latitude for the teacher's creative input. The model is very generic in structure, and can be used with any genre, or combinations of genre. It can be used for a simple one-day lesson, on one aspect of a book, or for a larger unit of work. However, in any case, its use is intended to help the young reader read and integrate the ideas of the books with their life experiences, and then to extend those life experiences to the larger world. Although we are focusing on character and theme, the IIU can be used to focus on other literary structures of a book.

The IIU is intended as a guide for the teacher, not as a scripted lesson to be followed literally or too narrowly. The teacher, in developing instruction using the guide, should allow for discussion and tangential work that pertains

The Conceptual Background and Practical Ideas for the Instructional Goals 105

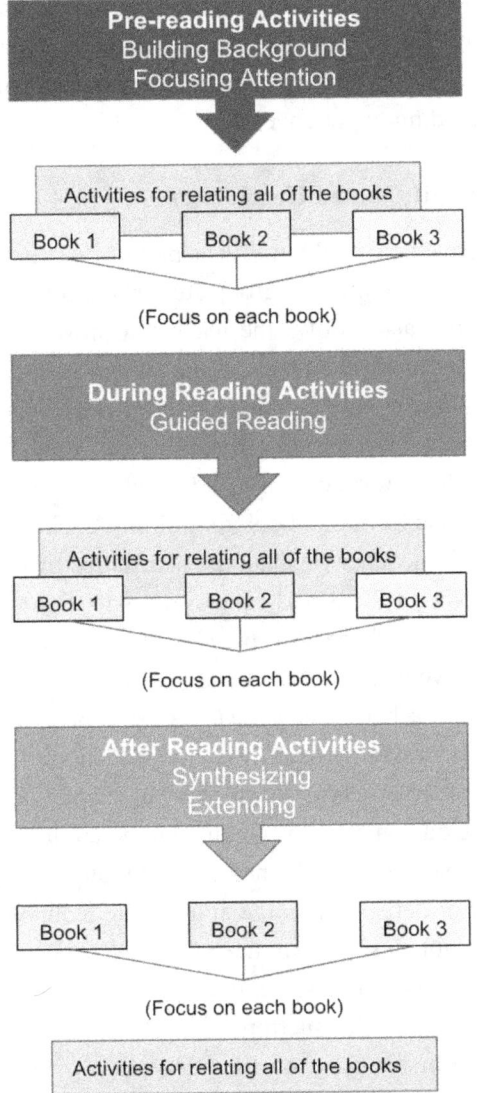

Figure 5.2. The Model for the Independent Instructional Unit (IIU).

to the theme, or variation of the theme, that is being developed through a variety of activities, both text-bound and extensions of the text.

As said earlier, the IIU can be a way for organizing the teacher's work, or it can be used by students to guide their own reading or the development of lessons for other students to follow. By extending its use to guide the student development of ways to guide reading, we believe that we have found a way to heighten the young reader's ability to share their understanding of the book and literature in general with others, either classmates or, what we may wish to call, bookmates. We believe that it can lead to better independence in a reader's lifelong reading experiences.

Creativity, Flexibility, and Effectiveness

The model has a great deal of flexibility as part of its structure. The structure allows for any number of ways to group students and to assign books to the groups. The structure also allows the teacher to have a different focus for instruction depending upon the needs of the student and the appropriateness of the book. It also discourages developing scripted lessons for the books that are being read. We believe that this flexibility not only helps the teacher's planning but also allows for more enjoyable exchanges in classwork and dialogue. The IIU can use from one book to multiple books for a lesson.

The IIU allows the teacher to shape the substance of instruction in many ways while still giving a focus and cohesiveness to the instruction of one or several books. It does not force a scripted lesson on the instruction so that the teacher can be creative in the instructional approach.

The IIU allows the teacher to apply the ideas for helping the reader find meaning in the book or books being read. It is an application of the ideas from the continuum model presented earlier in this text in chapter. The IIU encourages the intention and the outcomes of the continuum model. It has the role of developing in-depth understanding and higher-order thinking in obtaining meaning.

The IIU can use or depend upon the appropriate technology in ways to be illustrated in the sample lessons you have. It is the concepts of the books not the technology that drives the instruction. We will illustrate both the IIU and mini-lesson integrated with instruction.

Having given the background on the IIU, we now move on to illustrate what instruction would look like relative to the two facets of the theme of identity that we use to organize the work.

THE ARGUMENTS FOR THE CHOICES OF THEMES FOR OUR ILLUSTRATIONS OF APPROACHES

We already have made an argument for our choice of themes in chapters 1 and 2, but we wish to reinforce the relevance of these themes by tying them to the primary problems and the concerns of the young adult. We accomplish this goal through the sample lessons that follow.

SAMPLE LESSONS FOR THE IIU AND THE PROCESS FOR DEVELOPING THE IIU

Sample units and lessons to illustrate the flexibility and the structure of the model are presented here. We have selected several focal points for developing different aspects of the theme of identity, with a focus on identity and growth concerns. We have chosen these focal points because we believe that they are at the heart of the concerns of young adults. They also carry forward into later years as even adults change and grow as their lives change and present new situations that must be tested or adapted to.

The sample lessons here use multiple books by the same author, one book focused on key characteristics, one graphic novel to illustrate technology in a mini-lesson, and two books with similar themes for use with student-developed work.

The Process for Developing the IIU

This section of the chapter describes how teachers can develop the ideas and the structures for the IIU. It focuses on the thought and the development process for creating various forms of the IIU. It is not the only way to develop the IIU but does give someone new to this type of planning something to start with to do such work. The process is illustrated within the sample lesson.

The work presented here on the IIU is only a part of the chapter to illustrate the major aspects of instruction. There are additional parts of the chapter that will illustrate other aspects of instruction as can be seen by the full outline presented earlier. They are the mini-lessons, the student-developed work, and finally the process for developing all of this type of work.

The IIU: Sample with Multiple Texts by One Author—S. E. Hinton

The primary sample of the IIU that we give to you is with the use of three books by the same author, S. E. Hinton.

Three Novels by S. E. Hinton: "The Outsiders," "That Was Then, This Is Now," and "Tex"

Our decision to include an IIU, which highlights the importance of an author, is deliberate. We obviously share a belief in the power of individual novels and stories. We also share a belier in the important place authors can have within readers' lives. Oftentimes, readers are initially attracted to an author because of a specific book; however, as readers explore multiple books by the same author, the author's style, characters, themes, and voice reverberate with the readers' minds and hearts. Studying several books by the same author can provide readers with the sustained engagement that they often seek. This thinking directs our use of the three books by S. E. Hinton in the sample IIU.

Pre-Reading: Building Background for the Work and Giving a Focus to the Work of Studying Multiple Novels by One Author

The first guiding principle when approaching a study of multiple books by the same author is fidelity to the importance of personal response and engagement. According to Rosenblatt (1978), "We peel off layer after layer of concerns brought to bear—social, biographical, historical, linguistic, textual—and at the center we find the inescapable transactional events between readers and texts" (p. 175)

There are many valid approaches teachers can adopt to introduce the novels of S. E. Hinton. Given that S. E. Hinton started to write her first and most popular novel, *The Outsiders*, at the age of fifteen, there is a natural affinity young people often feel with Hinton.

Hinton based the events in *The Outsiders* on events that occurred in her high school in Tulsa, Oklahoma. Although Hinton was not a member of a gang, she had friends who were members of the "greasers". Hinton describes the rivalry between two gangs, the lower middle-class "greasers" and the upper-class "socs," and the conflict that leads to the deaths of members of both gangs. *The Outsiders* explores the friendship, loyalty, and affection in the gangs while simultaneously pointing out both the similarities in the feelings of the opposing groups and the uselessness of gang violence.

Sharing some biographical information about S. E. Hinton can help students activate their own background knowledge necessary for exploration of themes such as identity, family, belonging, and friendship. Teachers can help students delve deeply into these themes by encouraging students to reflect on their own personal experiences. Some suggested opening questions to encourage reflection are as follows:

> *What place do friends and family have in your life? In what ways do poverty and social and economic status dictate how others perceive you? What impact does gun violence have in your life? In what ways do events in your life shape the development of your character? Do you feel like an outsider in life?*

These types of questions help students begin to consider many of the themes present in all three of Hinton's books: identity, friendship, peer pressure, family, violence, and maturity. Thinking about the presence of Hinton's themes in their own lives helps students to relate to each of Hinton's three novels.

During Reading: Guiding the Reading and Related Work, and Directing Student and Teacher Discussions

A second guiding principle when approaching a study of multiple books is understanding that aesthetic response must precede response to literary elements.

A general statement such as "Think about something that happens in the story that reminds you of something that has happened in your own life" has the power to evoke an aesthetic response. Encouraging a personal, aesthetic response helps both students and teachers understand the potential literature has to touch readers' lives in a very personal way. This first opening statement can be presented prior to the reading of each of the three novels.

Following a discussion of the opening statement that invites personal response, we suggest that teachers then facilitate a discussion based on literary elements such as plot, character, theme, setting, or other characteristic. Although it may be tempting to focus on several literary elements, we recommend focusing on one or two. The underlying guiding principle is the belief that exploration of these one or two literary elements will deepen the students' literary and personal experience of a novel. The following is an example of a way to guide a discussion about character.

Guiding students to be able to evaluate a character's traits, their role in the story, and their response to the conflicts in the story will help enhance the reader's understanding of not only the characters in the novel but also of the themes. In order to analyze a character a teacher must encourage and model for students how to think critically, ask questions, and draw conclusions.

In these three novels, it is clear that Hinton focuses on individual characters. For example, in *The Outsiders* rather than portray The Greasers as a group, Hinton focuses on constructing characters such as Ponyboy, Sodapop, Darry, Johnny, and Dally. Ponyboy Curtis, the youngest member of The Greasers, narrates the novel. Below are some questions that will help students understand both the process of character analysis and the importance of character development within a novel.

The questions can be given to the student prior to either whole-class or small-group discussion either during the reading or following the reading of the book. This will help provide time for the students to think about their responses to ensure that there is adequate reflection. What follows are questions for each of the three Hinton books.

Book One: The Outsiders

At the beginning of the book, Ponyboy dislikes the Socs. "What is the basis for this dislike?" During the novel he realizes that the Socs, as well as the Greasers, have problems. "Which specific events lead Ponyboy to this change of attitude? How does this realization change Ponyboy's view of life?" These questions focus on the relationship and effect of events that cause change in a character's life. The following questions extend this goal. "Can you point out specific events which contribute to Ponyboy's struggles with class divisions, violence, innocence, and familial love? What comments by Johnny and Dally help change the way Ponyboy views Dally? In what ways does Ponyboy mature over the course of the novel? What does he eventually realize regarding the role violence plays in individual lives?"

Ponyboy likes to read. "By giving Ponyboy an appreciation of literature, what assumption is Hinton challenging with regard to how we view adolescents who are poor?"

"What do we learn about Ponyboy through the allusion to Robert Frost's poem 'Nothing' and Ponyboy's identification with Dicken's character Pip from the novel *Great Expectations*?" How do these questions help us to see Ponyboy differently?

Book Two: That Was Then, This Is Now

Again, giving students the questions at the appropriate time in the reading process helps ensure that students will engage in meaningful reflection.

This novel features two best friends, Bryon and Mark. Mark is also the younger adopted brother of Bryon. The novel opens in a pool hall. Looking at their behavior at the beginning of the novel, describe Mark and Bryon's idea of fun. "What effect does M & M's disapproving comments have on Bryon and Mark?"

While visiting their mother, who is in the hospital, Mark and Bryon meet Mike, the survivor of a vicious attack. "What impact does Mike's attitude and forgiveness of the attacker have on Bryon and Mark?"

As the novel unfolds, a series of violent incidents motivated by revenge leaves M & M in the hospital and Charley dead. Describe the different ways Mark and Bryon respond to the violence. "What in Bryon's attitude indicates that he is maturing and growing apart from Mark?"

At the end of the novel, Bryon calls the police and Mark is arrested for the possession of drugs. Although this seems to be the right thing to do, Bryon is overcome with guilt when Mark is arrested. "How does Bryon react to his guilt for calling the police on Mark? Who does Bryon unfairly blame for Mark's imprisonment? Is this a realistic response? What other ways could Bryon have chosen to respond?"

"How has the message Hinton explored in *The Outsiders* relating to innocence changed in *That Was Then, This Is Now*?"

Book Three: Tex

Again, considering when to present and distribute question encourages meaningful reflection. The novel begins with the conflict between fourtee -year-old Tex, the protagonist, and his brother, seventeen-year-old Mason. Their father is absent, and their mother is dead, so Mason bears the responsibility for caring for the two of them. Tex comes home from school and finds that Mason has sold both Negrito, Tex's beloved horse, and Red, his own horse. "Why did Mason sell the horses? What insight do the response of Tex and Mason provide into their characters?"

Later on, in the novel, Tex and his friend Johnny attend a party. Although they didn't mean to, they both get drunk. The next day Johnny's father accuses both Tex and Mason of being a negative influence on his children. "What does this scene show you about the way Tex and Mason are perceived by others? As future events unfold, what are the reasons for the change in Johnny's father's attitude toward Tex?"

Toward the end of the novel Tex and Mason's father reveals that Tex is not his biological son. This news results in a series of violent incidents. "What does Tex learn about himself and Mason?"

At the end of the novel, Tex and Jamie resume a positive relationship. Mason is accepted into college and Tex is given a job working with horses. "Do you believe that Hinton's character development of Tex and Mason supports this ending?"

After Reading: Synthesis of Work and Extension of the Reading and Discussion

Many of the above questions focus on character. By choosing to focus on the literary element of character we want the readers to first focus their reading on the characters in the text, and then move to broader concerns. Learning more about the character's development by analyzing their actions and decisions can lead students to identifying and articulating wider perspectives that reflect the meaning of the text. After reading the three novels, students should respond to questions that help them reflect on Hinton's novels as a body of work.

Which of your perspectives on life have been validated by the events of the novels?
Are there any ways in which your perspectives on life have been challenged?
Compare the endings of the three novels. In what ways has the message evolved? In what ways do you find each ending to be either realistic or unrealistic? Considering the sociological impact of groups on identity, what insights have you gained regarding the ways your friends and family impact your identity?
Which character traits several characters share? Which traits do you find admirable? Which traits do you hope to nurture within yourself?

Discuss Hinton's writing style. In what ways does her style reflect the theme of identity?

We believe that readers respond to literature in multiple ways. We also believe that encouraging personal response and increasing awareness of academic aspects of literature deepens understanding. When a teacher nurtures the reciprocity between personal response and academic learning, these two areas work together to enhance meaning.

A student's personal response can impact the way they view literary elements and can often lead to a change in personal response. When teachers include students in their understanding of the interplay between the personal and academic dimensions of reading, understanding is enhanced.

The IIU: Sample Lesson with One Book—Orphan Train

The next sample lesson is one of one book of historical fiction to show how the IIU can work for fewer than multiple books, and still be effective as a guide for instruction. Like the first sample with Hinton's books, we see the flexibility of the IIU and the ability to integrate concepts from the Continuum of Engagement, Transaction, and Understanding Model.

ORPHAN TRAIN BY CHRISTINA BAKER KLINE

This IIU designed for *Orphan Train* highlights an example of a work of fiction that creates a story rooted in facts. *Orphan Train* transforms historical facts into an emotional, compelling story of individuals struggling against tremendous adversity while grappling with feelings of loneliness, loss, and abandonment. This novel is an excellent example of historical fiction that is accessible to the young adult reader.

Pre-Reading: Building Background for the Work and Guiding a Focus to the Work

When writing *Orphan Train*, Kline researched this little-known part of American History. Although Kline's book is fictional, it is based on the true history of thousands of children shipped to the Midwest. Kline's inspiration for this novel was found in her own family; her husband's grandfather, Frank Robertson, traveled on an orphan train.

Between 1854 and 1929, "orphan trains" transported more than 200,000 orphaned, abandoned, and homeless children from the coastal cities of the eastern United States to the Midwest for "adoption." Like her husband's grandfather, many of these children were first generation Irish Catholic immigrants.

Her research also led her to a collection of letters housed at the New York Public Library. There she found many heartbreaking letters. The historical facts and the personal stories expressed in these letters are both present in this novel about the relationship between two strong women. Molly Ayer is a troubled seventeen-year-old foster child who has moved from one home to another. Vivian is a ninety-one-year-old widow who began her life in a village on the coast of Ireland, left the poverty of Ireland and emigrated with her family to a tenement in New York City, traveled on an orphan train to the Midwest, and eventually to a life in Minnesota. Both women share a journey filled with longing, neglect, abuse, and resilience.

Sharing some historical information about this period of history as well as information about Kline's research will help students activate their own background knowledge necessary for exploration of themes such as identity, immigration, family, loss, trust, and hope. Some suggested opening questions to encourage reflection are as follows:

In what ways can historical events such as The Great Depression shape individual lives?
How are the hopes of our immigrant parents, grandparents, and great grandparents similar to the hopes of current immigrants?
In what ways can the lack of a stable home and family impact a young person?
What types of behavior might young people learn when they are continually moved from house to house?
What fears might young people have before meeting a "potential" adoptive family?

These types of questions help students begin to consider many of the themes present in *Orphan Train* such as identity, immigration, family, loss, trust, resilience, and maturity. Thinking about the presence of these themes in their own lives helps students to relate to *Orphan Train*.

During Reading: Guiding the Reading and Related Work and Directing Student and Teacher Discussions

A general statement such as "Think about something that happened in the story that reminds you of something that has happened in your own life" has the power to evoke an aesthetic response. Encouraging a personal, aesthetic response helps both students and teachers understand the potential literature has to touch readers' lives in a very personal way. This first opening question can be asked several times during the reading.

In the pre-reading section, the teacher has set the stage for students to explore the literary elements of theme. Guiding students as they identify the many themes in this novel will enhance the reader's understanding not only of themes but also of the importance of setting and character.

Below are some questions that will help students understand the many ways theme, setting, and characters are interwoven throughout the novel. The questions can be given to the students prior to the whole-class or small-group discussion or during the reading or following the reading of the book. This will help provide time for the students to think about their response to ensure that there is adequate reflection.

What do you think of the "Orphan Trains"? Given the realities of The Great Depression, can you think of better options?

What similarities and differences are there between the practice of "Orphan Trains" and our current foster care system?

What similarities do Molly and Vivian share and what are some differences between these two women?

For these two women, their names are significant. Vivian was born Niamh Power, but over the course of her life her name was changed to Dorothy Nielsen and to Vivian Daly. Why is this significant? What is the significance of Molly Ayer's name? In what ways does Molly's name serve to hide her Indian heritage?

What role does silence and fear have in both Molly's life and in Vivian's life?

Create a time line of Vivian's life. How would you describe and characterize each segment of her life?

Imagine Milly's future and create a time line of her life. How would you describe and characterize each segment of her life?

How have Molly and Vivian changed each other's lives? Discuss the ways the literary elements of setting, character, and theme are interwoven throughout the book.

After Reading: Synthesis of work and Extension of the Reading and Discussion

The concept of "portaging" is central to this novel. Molly first hears about portaging in her American History class. "Portaging" refers to when "in the old days the Wabanki Indians had to carry their canoes and everything else they possessed across land from one water body to the next, so they had to think carefully about what to keep and what to discard" (Kline, 2013, p. 181). Molly's teacher, Mr. Reed, assigns his students the task of interviewing someone about their "portages."

Have the students reread the section in *Orphan Train* about "portaging" and then discuss the ways "portaging" is interwoven throughout the novel.

Following a discussion about "portaging," ask students to interview a person in their lives such as a parent or grandparent, about their "portages." Students should follow the directions Mr. Reed provided Molly and her classmates and use tape recorders and conduct what he calls "oral histories," asking the person questions, transcribing answers, and putting it together in chronological order as a narrative.

The questions are "What did you choose to bring with you to the next place? What did you leave behind? What insights did you gain about what's important?" (Kline, 2013, p. 131).

Students should be encouraged to include drawings or other visual representations of the "portaging." Students should be invited to share their "portaging" projects with each other so that comparisons between the characters in *Orphan Train* and the people in the students' lives can be made. When conversations such as these happen, understanding is enhanced, and the literary experience is deepened.

It is worth noting that the Afterword in the book contains a section entitled "A Short History of the Orphan Trains." This section contains historical information and photographs about this relatively unknown period of American History. The Afterword also includes an interview with the author, Christine Baker Kline, in which she shares her research. This is a valuable resource for student to begin to understand the ways in which nonfiction can impact fiction.

THE IIU: SAMPLE WITH GRAPHIC NOVEL FOR MINI-LESSONS

Often a teacher wants to emphasize one literary aspect of a book rather than the primary concepts of the entire books. The mini-lesson can serve that purpose. The mini-lesson also can be useful for introducing or using a type of technology to instruct in a relevant, meaningful way.

Mini-Lesson: Description, Value, and Use

Mini-lessons are lesson plans that focus on one aspect of the text, literary characteristics, a subtheme, or some type of technology. They can take as little as fifteen minutes, or one or two class periods. The goal is to have students gain background, or to look closely at one small part of the work related to the book. It can serve as any part of the IIU (pre-reading, during reading, after reading) where a complete IIU is not appropriate or needed. It can give clarity to a specific characteristic of a book when the book uses a specific technique to deliver its meaning. It may illustrate something specific about a writer's style as it manifests itself in a book.

This section of the chapter describes how teachers can develop and use mini-lessons in effective ways. To the extent possible, we give step-by-step guides for developing mini-lessons. When developing a mini-lesson that centers around students using technology, it is important to remember that they may not be familiar with the particular software, application, or digital tool you are asking them to use.

Before you can approach the content, you must do a mini-lesson on how to use the particular technology. Ideally, you should structure the lesson to include a brief introduction to the tool and what it does, followed by a short demonstration. Leave some time for students to ask questions, and then allow them the remainder of the class to explore the tool. As students add technical skills to their toolkit, such as blogging or using a tool such a Flipgrid, you will be able to jump straight into the content of texts for future mini-lessons.

A Sample Lesson and the Process for Developing a Mini-Lesson with Technology

Technology can be a particularly useful tool for researching information, especially during pre-reading activities when students are learning about the historical, cultural, or geographical context of a text. In this sample lesson, students are working on pre-reading activities for the graphic novel *The Complete Persepolis* by Marjane Satrapi, which tells Satrapi's story of growing up in Tehran during the Iranian Revolution.

Many of today's students will be unfamiliar with the Iranian Revolution. Though it would be easy to introduce them to the history through a mini-lesson, the students will be more likely to engage with and remember the information if they complete their own research. However, it is important that they understand how to conduct a meaningful Internet search that yields reliable results.

These pre-reading activities should be completed over several class sessions. Begin with introducing students to the book and ask them what they already know about the Iranian Revolution, what they know about Iran, and have them write down questions they would like to answer. Then launch into your mini-lesson about how to use Google for effective Internet research. You can first demonstrate how to enter search strings to get specific results, and then discuss with the class the importance of using credible sources for their research.

The Center for Media Literacy suggests five key questions one should ask when evaluating an information source:

- Who created this message? And why?
- Who is the target audience?
- How have economic decisions influenced the construction of this message?
- What reasons might an individual have for being interested in this message?
- How might different individuals interpret this message differently?

Introduce and explain these questions, and then demonstrate to students how to evaluate sources using this framework. Remind students that they can apply these questions to any form of media—text, photographs, audio, video, animation, and so on.

When you are finished with the mini-lesson, students should conduct Google searches to find the answers to the questions they came up with at the

The Conceptual Background and Practical Ideas for the Instructional Goals 119

beginning of class. They can bookmark sites they find useful and begin the process of evaluating their credibility.

During the next class session, introduce students to the group work they will be doing—curating information about the Iranian Revolution and creating a Google Slideshow (or PowerPoint presentation) that answers the following questions:

Where is Iran?
When was the Iranian Revolution?
How long did it last?
Who was involved, and why?
What was the cause?
What was the end result?

If you have not used webjets (http://webjets.io) with students for past classwork, use this mini-lesson to introduce them to this particular web tool that essentially turns anything you add to it into virtual sticky notes or index cards, which you can visually arrange and organize. This includes text, audio, video, and more. Once you have completed the demonstration, allow students to return to their bookmarked sites and begin curating content.

You may need to do a third mini-lesson if students are not familiar with Google Slides or PowerPoint, otherwise, they can use the remainder of the classes dedicated to this pre-reading activity to curating information and creating their slideshow.

This mini-lesson contains teacher-directed and student-directed work. The next section focuses on student-developed work.

STUDENT-DEVELOPED WORK: THE USE OF STUDENT-DEVELOPED WORK AS A MEANS FOR INSTRUCTION AND RATIONALE FOR THIS WORK

Teachers do not need to do all of the teaching. It can be very effective having students develop plans for their own study of a text. This section describes how to guide students to develop lessons for themselves as well as for their peers. Slowly, this approach to instruction shifts responsibility for learning to the student. There are several things that drive student-developed work. They are giving up control, allowing individuals to work both independently and cooperatively in a collaborative process in groups.

Giving Up Control—Shifting Responsibility for Learning

It is difficult for teachers to give up control. Sometimes there seems to be a loss of efficiency. However, giving up control seems to be at the heart of using student-developed lessons. It encourages students to think about a book from multiple perspectives, particularly as a teacher does. Students then can refocus their personal perspective to consider the perspective of others.

Individuals

Students can work independently in doing their work as a way to guide their own study, or to plan a presentation on some aspect of the coursework. This section describes and illustrates how to do that type of work. Students may generate their own purposes and pre-reading and post-reading questions or activities. They may develop journals of their reflections and insights as a basis for further activities to support reading the text or to extend their thinking and activities beyond the text.

Collaboration and Group-Generated Work

Collaboration is an important part of helping students to negotiate and share ideas and multiple perspectives on a text. This section illustrates how to do this work. We include it because we believe that it encourages a synthesis of the ideas that each student brings to the tasks.

Sample of Student-Developed Work Guidelines

After teachers have used the IIU model and mini-lesson guidelines for class instruction a few times it may be appropriate to shift responsibility for learning to the students. Doing so can be done several ways. However, we suggest the initial attempts be done with groups of four students working together and following the IIU model and mini-lesson guidelines to develop instruction for their fellow classmates. This does mean that the teacher will need to relinquish some control of the work; however, there is often much to be gained from this process.

The sample that follows uses two books: one a classic, the other a contemporary one. The books are *A Separate Peace* by John Knowles written in 1959 and *Aristotle and Dante Discover the Secrets of the Universe* by Benjamin Alire Saenz written in 2012.

Before describing the general process for student-developed work we will give you a summary of each book. It should be noted, that although the two books have male characters as their protagonists, the books and the development of the student-developed lesson should help young adults of all genders understand more fully the underlying struggles of young adult relationships. A parallel lesson can be done with female and/or nonbinary protagonists if the teacher feels a need to balance the gender concern.

A Separate Peace is set in New England during the early years of World War II. Two adolescents, Gene and Phineas, are the main characters of a look at the dark side of adolescence that moves two very different boys from innocence into a more difficult time of adulthood. At the heart of the novel is the exploration of true friendship.

Aristotle and Dante Discover the Secrets of the Universe takes place at a later time with different kinds of characters than those in *A Separate Peace*. However, it too explores the nature of the bonds of two young boys in a moving coming-of-age story. Their struggle reflects the hurdles their relationship faces in the time and the place where they live.

Directing the Student Group Process

1. Have the students read both books and make reflective notes of their thoughts and responses, both affective and intellectual, to the stories characters, problems, and themes as the students see them.
2. Then, leave the groups to their own discussions about the books based upon their individual notes.
3. Next, ask them to select a leader, a recorder, and a reporter. The discussion and the record of the discussion should focus on the group's development of an IIU and a related mini-lesson. In doing so, they need to decide how they will work and what their objectives are for the lesson.
4. They should proceed to work as they plan for the next week to week and a half to complete the work that they will present to the class, perhaps sharing their work online.

5. The teacher needs to remove themself from the process around step two and allow the students to work through and address any problems that they face doing the assignment on their own.
6. Class presentations should not exceed twenty minutes for each group. Once the presentations have been completed, the teacher can lead a full class discussion on the approaches that each group took, and what they learned from doing the work this way as well as the ideas from the book.
7. The hope is that student will have assimilated and incorporated some of the views that we are presenting in this book for reading young adult literature and show how this enhances their reading.

SUMMING UP

Chapter 5 has given you the thinking that guides our suggestions for several approaches to instruction. The guidelines included a model for an IIU, a mini-lesson, and a process for implementing student-developed work. In this chapter we have given sample lessons to illustrate each of these approaches. The samples take different directions depending upon the actual books selected to illustrate different instructional objectives. The hope is that teachers will find these samples useful for designing their own instruction and creating a good learning environment in their classrooms.

Chapter 6

Final Remarks and Implications for the Implementation of Curriculum Organization and Content

OVERVIEW OF CHAPTER 6

Chapter 6 addresses the implications of the perspectives, ideas, and specific suggestions made in chapters 1 through 5. This chapter identifies several key points that can be derived from the earlier chapters in the book, beginning with concepts related to the transformation of young adulthood. This chapter accomplishes the goal of addressing the implications of the ideas in the book by looking at how school districts, individual schools, teachers, and students are influenced by these implications. To some degree, the chapter illustrates the implications at each of these levels of educational endeavors so that teachers can see the effect of the perspective of this book on their professional responsibilities and work. The chapter also tries to show how this perspective may change or challenge students to learn differently and achieve important thinking abilities related to reading literature—specifically young adult literature.

QUESTIONS GUIDING THE READING

What are the key ideas from chapters 1 through 5 that will have major implications for curriculum, instruction, and learning?

What do school districts and individual schools need to consider when implementing the ideas from chapters 1 through 5?

What do the ideas and suggestions from chapters 1 through 5 mean for the classroom teacher?

What does this perspective mean for students' responsibilities for their learning?

If the implications require rethinking district objectives and procedures, school curriculum and practices, teachers' perspectives, and student learning, how do you accomplish these changes and challenges?

KEY IDEAS FROM CHAPTERS 1 THROUGH 5

The key ideas derived from chapters 1 through 5 fall into four categories with several points within each category. These categories are as follows:

1. The effect of the transformation of young adults on their identity development.
2. The instructional and assessment concerns related to young adult literature.
3. The overall implications for implementation of the ideas presented here.
4. Decision, commitment, planning, and implementation concerns.

All of these ideas have implications for addressing and implementing the ideas presented in this book.

In this first category of important points, we are suggesting two major effects of the transformation of young adults on their identity development. First, we need an understanding of this transformation with regards to literary, psychological, and sociological perspectives. We need to understand how each of these perspectives has distinctly different effects on identity development, and why that is important to the teaching of young adults and of young adult literature. Second, we need to understand how this transformation influences curriculum, instruction, and learning relative to the use of young adult literature.

For the second category we need to address instructional and assessment concerns for the curriculum and the classroom. To accomplish this goal we need to consider suggestions for incorporating the effective strategies and the use of technology in instruction and assessment. Further, we need to broaden our view to include not only the assessment of young adults' understanding of literature but also the assessment of strategies that encourage lifelong reading.

For the third category we need to identify overall implications for each level of educational endeavor, such as district, school, teacher, parent, and student levels, on developing young adults' ability to become critical, reflective thinkers as a result of reading young adult literature.

The fourth category of major points focuses on the implications of the ideas from chapters 1 through 5 on decisions, commitments, planning, and implementation for districts, schools, teachers, parents, and students. Here we need to consider planning guidelines for the implementation of all ideas for curriculum and instruction by considering selection of materials and content, instructional approaches, integration into subject area instruction, use of classic and contemporary selections, and finally, the role of libraries and librarians. We also examine the role of all of the stakeholders in decision-making and the implementation of ideas and the plans.

Although we attempt to highlight these concerns within each of the four categories separately, some of the concerns are integrated across the sections across the four categories.

Transformation in Young Adulthood

There needs to be an understanding of the transformative period of young adulthood as it relates to the development of identity from literary, psychological, and sociological perspectives. All three perspectives bring to bear the theoretical frameworks that point to the development of one's identity as central to this stage of growth. They also strongly suggest that this is the stage of greatest influence by peers, society, and internal retrospection. This suggests many changes in the young adult's sense of who they are psychologically and sociologically. Young adult readers may even see their roles in life change as they accept new responsibilities in young adulthood. From a literary perspective, they also are more likely to understand aspects of literature that help them to see multiple points of view as they are expressed in a narrative.

Often, this transformation causes personal confusion for the young adult. Because of this confusion, young adults are trying to answer the questions "Who am I?" and "What will I become?" They are doing this with regards to personal identities as well as defining their ability to accomplish societal and personal expectations and goals. The books that they read at this time must speak to these concerns for the reader to acknowledge the book's value and relevance.

Second, there needs to be an understanding of how this transformation influences curriculum, instruction, and learning through the use of young adult literature. This transformation influences what they are reading to learn personally and intellectually in a way that contributes to growth. It often influences what they are interested in learning through their reading and thinking individually and with their peers. Those who determine the goals for reading literature of any type need to see how their decisions determine the content of curriculum as well as how the choices for forms and strategies for instruction influence the learning that takes place.

The educator's decisions with regard to these factors needs to recognize the high importance of helping the young adult engage in the reading. Young adult literature helps with this goal, and serves as a transition to reading more complex literature with more mature representation of themes in the human experience. The hope also is that reading young adult literature helps young adults mature and develop broader understandings of human lives beyond their own experience.

Instructional and Assessment Concerns

We also need to consider suggestions for incorporating effective strategies and the use of technology into instruction with young adults and young adult literature. Effective strategies must engage the young adult readers so that they feel what they read has immediate relevance in their lives. This often means making abstract work very concrete and direct. It does not mean that older classic texts are to be dismissed. Instead, teachers need to assist students in seeing the relevance of these classic texts in a way that acknowledges the young adult's skills and life experiences.

Students also have grown up in a different environment where much of their communication is through technological venues. So, their processing of text may differ from what their teachers are accustomed to. They also may be more familiar with alternative ways of learning beyond a straightforward reading of a text.

Educators need to consider a variety of strategies of instruction and assessment to tap the young adults' processing and understanding of the message of a text. In general, concrete, active interactions are more successful at this stage of development. This type of instruction also prepares the young adult for more abstract, reflective reading required by more complex text.

This understanding also prompts a reconsideration of the types of assessment that we do.

Thus, we need to address issues related to the assessment of reading ability, particularly as related to understanding young adult literature and lifelong learning through reading young adult literature.

While updated standardized tests give us reasonable large population comparative norms, they are bound by specific mathematical assessment models that are limited culturally and intellectually to narrow perceptions on cognition and literacy. Too often standardized tests have only assessed easily measurable performance in reading without addressing many of the concerns we have presented here. The assessments generally focus on literary and intellectual concerns with regards to basic performance around traditional culturally established norms and reading selections.

Our concern about reading literature and developing insightful understanding of the meaning of the text as Rosenblatt defines aesthetic reading prompts us to reconsider this view as the only way to measure performance. Multiple forms of assessment to tap the insight and emotional response evoked by the reading of literature may be needed. "What form they should take is the key question here? What determines the model for that type of assessment?"

The appropriate assessment of literacy for young adult readers needs to be developed at district and school levels if young adult literature is part of the core of the curriculum and needs to be beyond standardized tests. This need to consider multiple levels/types of assessment for evaluating student and school performance also needs to be tied to the instructional strategies that we have suggested are useful for young adults. We also need to ask, "How can we use technology to accomplish this task?" because instructional strategies that we use will influence the type of assessment that we do. There are four concerns to address these questions.

First, the instructional strategies that we use will influence the type of learning and the type of assessment that transpire relative to achieving and measuring in-depth understanding of text. The first two of our concerns, transformation along with instruction and assessment, will need to be reflected in these additional forms of assessment.

Next, it appears as though we may need a *Four Tier Model for Assessment* to accomplish the goal of a broader view of assessing a reader's understanding of a text. The four levels may be as follows:

1. Standardized tests that incorporate young adult literature and the evaluation of the text thus evaluating the cognitive aspects of the process
2. A way to assess the affective, aesthetic, and insightful responses to the text thus assessing the less visible underlying aspects of the reading process
3. The reading habits of young adults
4. The integration of the virtual learning environment in instruction and assessment

This model for assessment then must be part of the overall implications of all levels of the educational endeavor.

Finally, we also may find that once teachers understand the use of the many emerging technologies, we can enhance the way that we assess literature to incorporate the reading strategies young adults use to read in a virtual learning environment. Accomplishing these goals may require teachers and students to alter their preconceived notions of what is involved in the reading of young adult literature.

The following *Four Tier Model for Assessment* attempts to represent this broadened view of the kind of assessment that we think is needed (figure 6.1).

Overall implications for all levels of educational endeavors
Implications at the district and school levels
District and individual schools level of commitment and openness to using young adult literature and incorporating technology into instruction and assessment

Part A: Assessment of Understanding		Part B: Assessment of Reader Behaviors	Part C: Ability to Work in a Virtual Learning Environment
Tier I	Tier II	Tier III	Tier IV
Standardized Test Form	Assessment of Affective, Aesthetic and Insightful Personal Responses	Reading Habits of Young Adult Readers	Application to Virtual Learning Environment
Cognitive Ability To Comprehend Ability to Evaluate A Text Inclusion of Young Adult Literature in Assessment Practices	Personal, Emotional Level Responses Literary, Psychological and Sociological Levels for Interpretation Creative, Unexpected Levels of Expression	School-related Habits Independent Reading-related Habits	Instructional and Learning Strategies Application to Assessment Process aligned with Instruction

Figure 6.1. **Four Tier Model for Assessment.**

Districts and schools in the district have to make a strong commitment to teaching literature of all types/genres to achieve the outcomes of literacy as given earlier in the book. This means extending the concept of literature beyond traditional fiction selections in the English classroom and beyond a curriculum that is focused only on limited subjects, culture contexts, and themes. It means that all genres have something to offer the young adult reader.

This commitment also needs to include determining the developmental level of the students in light of the concepts that we have presented earlier in this book. Our greatest concern is at the young adult reader level because we think the resistance to including books written for the young adult audience still is strong even with the change in the quality of those books.

Often once we get beyond the students in honors classes we lose many young readers because we remain very "high-minded" in selecting books. This practice leads to the young adult reader being deprived of the pleasure of a meaningful reading experience and being ill prepared for the traditional texts from earlier historical periods or from a standard curriculum. How do districts and schools make these commitments? Thus, there is a need to broaden the curriculum to do several things:

1. Acknowledge all genre types
2. Extend the range of themes and cultural representations in the selections
3. Extend the view that reading literature is simply an academic enterprise
4. Acknowledge that schools need to develop lifelong readers who attain the outcomes of literacy that we identified in the model of outcomes of literacy presented earlier in the book

Districts and schools in the district need to be open to using young adult literature in their curriculum for all types of readers so that relevant themes and issues of young adulthood are addressed. We also need to address how young adult literature and virtual learning can be gateways to reading for the young adult reader. The incorporation of both young adult literature and virtual learning acknowledge the social milieu of the day and what we accept about the development of young adults intellectually, psychologically, and sociologically as well as the changing nature of communication. Districts need to be open to incorporating virtual learning into the curriculum. The virtual community needs to be embraced and incorporated into the curriculum in a variety of ways. The themes and problems that we identified earlier are at the heart of young adult literature and the developmental stage of young adulthood.

The Individuals Making the Decisions: Who Are the Stakeholders?

Districts and schools need to identify who has input into decisions on these matters and make formal commitments to these decisions. School boards, district administrators, school administrators, parents, teachers, and students will all want a voice in making these decisions and be committed to carrying them out. How do we accomplish a stakeholder model in our schools?

Later in this chapter we describe "Learning Communities" as a way to initiate and carry out changes in the way the stakeholders view their work and decision-making with regards to teaching literature. The model suggests how these stakeholders can participate as integrated groups to understand the value of using young adult literature, the strategies that can be effective in instruction, and in alignment with the *Four Tier Model for Assessment* that we have proposed. Then formal decisions can be implemented in the schools.

The decisions that the stakeholders make given the interactive process they use will have implications for classroom teachers and students. The following sections address these implications.

The Implications for School Boards, School Districts, and Parents

This group of stakeholders needs to examine its role in setting goals for the students that they teach, and then work with teachers to develop reasonable guidelines and processes for developing curriculum for the students. Given the focus of the concerns of this book, they need to review how their decisions with regards to policies on curriculum, school organization, and assessment of progress influence instruction for young adult readers. The decisions this group makes must extend the work of previous grades and also prepare students for when they leave school either to go to further education or enter the workforce.

These stakeholders must believe that there is value in instruction based upon literature that is appropriate for young adults for these students to develop as individuals and become contributing critical thinking members of a democratic society. They also must be open to multiple types of assessment of students' success in reaching the goals set by the community and the nation as a whole. Without this commitment, any effort by teachers will not be successful.

The Implications for the Classroom Teacher

Teachers Need Freedom

Teachers are often required to follow curriculum guidelines and state standards. While this structure helps teachers assist students achieve certain measurable reading objectives, teachers should also be encouraged to make their own decisions regarding both the choice of novels and the choice of teaching strategies to engage students. Teachers also need to help students understand their own reading habits in relationship to schoolwork and to independent reading as a means to encourage lifelong readers.

Teachers should be encouraged to explore theoretical frameworks and models that validate not only the cognitive dimension of reading but also the experiential and personal aspects of the reading process. The combination of guidelines, standards, and theoretical frameworks should serve as the foundation for teachers to move forward to implement literature units.

Teachers Use of Young Adult Literature for the Classroom and Independent Reading

When teachers are encouraged to engage students through young adult novels, they are inviting students into the world of literature. For many students, this experience with young adult literature may be their first step into understanding the power of literature. It also is important for teachers to remember that as they assist students in understanding what it means to "live-through" texts and in gaining confidence in their own responses to literature, students are developing the literary background necessary to read more traditional literature.

Teachers should be encouraged to view young adult literature as powerful genre of literature that also has the potential to prepare students to read traditional, classical literature. Teachers should be encouraged to pair young adult literature with traditional books of similar themes. For example, a book such as *Aristotle and Dante Discover the Secrets of the Universe* could be paired with the more traditional novel such as *A Separate Peace*.

While both novels explore the question of identity, the more contemporary setting and tone of *Aristotle and Dante Discover the Secrets of the Universe* may help prepare students to read the more traditional novel *A Separate Peace*. The setting, both time and place, of *A Separate Peace* is central to its meaning. World War II serves as a backdrop for the reader to witness the ways characters deal with not only a military war but also a personal inner war. In both books characters struggle with who they are, and as students articulate the similarities and differences among the characters, the students will enhance their comprehension of the struggle for identity as it is shaped in different historical periods.

At the heart of teaching literature to adolescents is the belief that by experiencing stories, young people will develop not only intellectual stills but also a lifelong love of reading. Using young adult literature as the precursor to more complex novels can encourage this development because teachers can start with books that are more immediately relevant to the young adult and then prepare them conceptually for the more complex text.

When teachers skillfully engage students in meaningful discussion of novels, they are helping students develop their capacity to think critically and their capability to use their imaginations so that they can become intelligent, compassionate, and productive members of society. Through choosing books that students can connect with, teachers are assisting students in discovering the power, beauty, and the joy of literature. Within the process of engaging students with stories, teachers are embracing the belief that all students are entitled to experience the transformative power of literature.

In addition to the implications related to cognitive and affective engagement and responses to reading literature, particularly young adult literature, we have identified two other concerns in our *Four Tier Model for Assessment* that have implications for teachers.

First, discussions with students about their reading habits needs to be included in instruction and assessment so that students become aware of effective and ineffective strategies and behaviors that they have for reading literature. Such discussions can enhance students' ability to read with enjoyment and success with both cognitive and affective levels of understanding.

Second, as our forms of communication change and forms for presentation of literature change to include the virtual learning environment, teachers will need to learn and integrate aspects of the virtual learning environment into instruction and assessment. The virtual learning environment may have much to offer the experience of reading literature in ways teachers have not expected. This means that professional development may need to embrace this kind of training. We also may find ways to better assess our students' success with experiencing literature.

The Implications for Assessment Affecting All Stakeholders

Given the concerns of this book, the assessment of literacy needs to address the inclusion of young adult literature in the classroom as it relates to young adults. How do we assess the characteristics of young adult literature as defined earlier in this book? Can they simply be added to our assessment forms following the *Four Tier Model for Assessment* as a guide along with the theoretical views of individuals like Rosenblatt, Bloom, and Gardner?

We think that this broadened view of assessment can help make assessment more effective. To accomplish this goal the assessment of reading ability needs to be through multiple forms to assess reader's understanding of young adult literature. Why and what are the multiple forms that will work? How do these multiple forms align with district and school measures as well as with those measures that extend beyond school?

These questions need to be addressed in the "Learning Communities" we use to facilitate decision-making and planning. These multiple forms of assessment also need to be built into the *Four Tier Model for Assessment* Practices. The next section on professional development helps us see how these implications may be addressed.

Opportunities for Professional Development as a Vehicle for Change

Today's parents, teachers, politicians, and business people all offer suggestions to improve today's schools. Oftentimes the suggestions are conflicting and are motivated by political interests. Many times the proposed improvement plans focus on solutions such as a strong emphasis on standardized testing that are in direct contradiction to theories that focus on the individual nature of each reader and the uniqueness of the reading experience.

This text proposes that young adult literature has tremendous potential to positively impact students' intellectual, psychological, and social development. Yet, for the power of young adult literature to be realized in the classroom teachers and administrators need to embrace young adult literature as a powerful educational resource.

When educational practices need to be changed or improved, one primary vehicle for change is professional development for teachers. Although professional development often is regarded as the primary means to achieve change, the results are often described as ineffective (Rowell, 2007). Some reasons attributed to the ineffectiveness of professional development are the lack of support and lack of future follow-up for staff development as well as a lack of leadership among administration. It is also not surprising that the pressure created by an emphasis on testing leads to a hesitation by teachers to embrace strategies that are not directly related to students' test performances (Scott et al., 2009).

Given the complexity of our society and the diversity of our students as well as the political and the economic conditions of our time, the challenge teachers face to assist all of our students to become critical readers and effective writers is a daunting one. As educators we must understand that in order for us to meet this challenge instruction must have a dual focus: teachers must teach the students the skills necessary to access the texts that are presented and must simultaneously present works of literature in a way that engages students in thinking, experiencing, and discussing books so that they can better understand themselves, others, and the world that we live in.

Learning Communities

In addition to identifying conditions that impeded professional development, researchers have identified key elements of professional development that make change possible. One key element is a school's commitment to teamwork, where teachers, support staff, and administrators work together toward a common goal: "Teaching Learning Communities appear to be the most effective, practical method for changing day to day classroom practice" (Williams, 2007/2008, p. 39). This shift from top-down professional development to professional Learning Communities or study groups represents a shift that embodies collaboration and teamwork rather than an administrative imposition of teaching practices.

The idea of "Learning Communities" has tremendous potential as a means to encourage the use of young adult literature in the classroom. We believe that groups of parents, teachers, staff, and administrators who spend time experiencing and discussing young adult literature in a "book group" format will discover and rediscover the power of young adult literature. We also believe that if the literary experience is combined with the exploration of cognitive theories of learning such as Bloom's Taxonomy of Educational

Objectives and other theories such as Louise Rosenblatt's Theory of Aesthetic Response and Howard Gardner's Theory of Multiple Intelligences, the understanding of the theoretical framework will provide further evidence and support to use young adult literature as an effective classroom practice to strengthen students' intellectual, psychological, and social development.

Guidelines for Implementing a Young Adult Literature Learning Community

There are necessary conditions for a "learning community" to be effective (Williams, 2007/2008). The "learning community" must have both a compelling direction for its work and an enabling structure that supports learning from one another. Clearly, exploring strategies that provide opportunities for young adult literature to become a powerful influence in students' intellectual, psychological, and social development is a worthwhile goal.

Although the goal is focused, there are many possible ways to structure the sessions. Certain practical aspects of designing the structure involve determining a time frame, selecting participants, and designing an overall structure. Determining a time frame involves setting a time and date for both individual sessions and a time frame for which the entire project will occur. Time should also be allowed for participants to observe the modeling of strategies and receive feedback on the strategies used in their own classrooms. Selecting participants will involve making decisions related to both the number of participants and the position each participant has within the school system, for example, parents, teachers, staff, and administrators.

In order to choose an effective structure, thought must be given to designing a structure that supports the goals. Given that this book focuses on the experiential dimension of reading and the importance of the personal, aesthetic response, the structure of the "learning community" also should embody these components.

The following are suggestions related to designing a structure that supports the goals of this book:

1. In order to better understand the importance of experiencing literature, participants in the group should have the opportunity to experience literature. The experiential dimension of young adult literature is a central tenet of this book, and in order to assist students in developing the capacity to "live-through" books, this capacity must often be awakened

or reawakened in the adults. For one part of the learning community sessions, the structure of "literature circles" or "book groups" may be helpful. Reading and discussing young adult novels with group members will allow participants to rediscover the relevance, depth, and power of young adult literature.

2. Additionally, the exploration of the literature should be accompanied by a study of cognitive theories such as Bloom's Taxonomy of Educational Objectives. This study should provide participants with a review of the importance of both academic skills associated with literacy and the important role that standardized testing has in informing instruction.

3. Additionally, the exploration of the literature should be accompanied by a study of theories such as Louise Rosenblatt's Theory of Aesthetic Response and Howard Gardner's Theory of Multiple Intelligences. Examination and discussion of these theories will provide participants with further evidence and support to use young adult literature as an effective classroom practice that not only strengthens students' intellectual ability but also nurtures students' psychological and social development. These theories will also provide participants evidence of the importance of broadening the focus of the curriculum to include dimensions of reading such as the personal and aesthetic response to reading.

4. Attention also should be given to the Continuum of Engagement, Transaction, and Understanding Model (figure 2.1) discussed throughout this book. Considering this model as a visual representation that combines the cognitive, intellectual component of reading with the aesthetic dimension of reading is a helpful way for participants to realize that the cognitive dimensions of reading and the aesthetic, personal dimension of reading both need to be developed in order to maximize students' potential to realize the power of literature.

5. Training in reading behaviors and strategies from the perspective of the reader along with training in the integration of appropriate technology to incorporate aspects of the virtual learning environment need to be addressed.

6. Finally, training in multiple types of assessment practices is needed to complete implementation and success.

Perhaps, too, the persistent voices of researchers such as Latrise P. Johnson; Mollie V. Blackburn; Kelly Gallagher; the National Council of Teachers of English CARBTE (Committee Against Racism and Bias in the Teaching of English); and Lesbian, Gay, Bisexual, Transgender, and Queer Advisory

Committee members, as well as the teacher-researchers leading the movement to #DisruptTexts - Tricia Ebavaria, Lorena Germàn, Dr. Kimberly N. Parker, and Julia E. Torres (https://disrupttexts.org), will combine with effective professional development to transform the use of young adult literature in classrooms in order to help students become productive, compassionate, and thoughtful adults. Doing so, combined with the key ideas from this book, should help young adults engage in and understand deeply the books that they read.

The Implications for Students

The final goal and results for students rest with the development of engagement in literacy, taking self-responsibility, developing questions and self-evaluation, higher-order thinking, and reflection. These become the real objectives for literacy, specifically reading, that often are not easily measured on tests because the answers are variable in nature—not simply right or wrong but based upon words rather than meaning. Readers learn to feel and to think simultaneously, and then learn to separate the two types of responses more objectively. They need to be part of the assessment of student performance, perhaps guided by the Outcomes of Literacy Model we presented earlier.

Engagement in Literacy

Engagement issues and lifelong reading are reflected in the Continuum of Engagement, Transaction, and Understanding Model (figure 2.1) and Outcomes of Literacy Model (figure 1.5). Readers need to engage in the text at two levels—affective and intellectual. For many, without the affective, emotional level they are not sustained adequately to engage at an intellectual level. There are some readers who are engaged intellectually and who read the text differently from those who only engage affectively. They bring the literary, academic tools to the text. However, to benefit from the text they cannot be disengaged from the affective response because the depth of understanding rests in the intersection of both types of engagement the way the continuum model presented earlier represents them.

Taking Self-Responsibility

Self-responsibility for learning is the goal in shifting to guided student-developed learning. Over time the responsibility for learning must rest with the young adult readers to know how they can be engaged in a text. They need to learn to set their purposes for reading so that they experience both the affective and the intellectual responses needed to achieve the depth of understanding of concepts and themes presented in the text. This gives the text its richness of meaning and prompts discussion of conflicting views. Students also need to learn how to be purposeful, yet flexible, when reading so that they experience and process a text to obtain deep understanding of a book.

Questions and Self-Evaluation

Developing one's own questions and self-evaluation of understanding of young adult literature is the key to developing effective behaviors as well as the strategies for achieving the goals of the Continuum of Engagement, Transaction, and Understanding Model (figure 2.1) and Outcomes of Literacy Model (figure 1.5). How and why do we accomplish this task? Young adult readers need to learn to find the unanswered question that a text presents to explore in-depth meaning of the text.

The reader also needs to learn to evaluate how well they have understood what the author may have said. This questioning process can lead to the reader's own growth and reflection on how the text is moving them to understand themself or others better. Has the reader, as a result of this questioning, understood the world a bit better too?

Higher-Order Thinking in Shaping One's Identity

Developing higher-order thinking and shaping one's identity becomes the student's responsibility. The nature and the complexity of the questions that students learn to raise can help them to delve deeply into themselves and shape their transformation into young adulthood. Discussion that leads to the upper ends of Bloom's Taxonomy, exploring texts as Rosenblatt encourages, and expanding the expression of understanding as Gardner suggests give students the space and place for this type of thinking. Without this level of thinking, reading literature does not give the student the understanding they need to really gain from the literature they read.

Reflective Reading

Developing reflective reading of young adult literature requires time to think about what one reads so that the nature of the young adult's reading process may change too. Its goal is no longer focused at a literal level—it looks to evaluate and to assimilate the deeper meaning of the text in relationship to life's universal themes and dilemmas. The pace of the reading may change to reflect the process of the reader's increased focus on reflecting on the nuances and the meaning within the text.

From the implications for districts, schools, teachers, and students we see an emergence of decisions, commitments, planning, and implementation guidelines for meeting our goals. They are the integration of young adult literature into subject areas, effective instruction, selection of content, and the role of libraries and resources for supporting the implementation of the ideas that develop.

Decisions, Commitments, Planning, and Implementation Guidelines for Curriculum Development and Instruction

"At what level do specific decisions get made? How does everyone involved demonstrate commitment? What is the impact on planning and implementation?" These questions need to be addressed for success in developing the kind of literacy we hope to develop through the reading of young adult literature. We believe that we can move in the right direction by identifying a few objectives, and having a strong commitment to implementing them.

Integrating Young Adult Literature and Technology into All Subjects

First, by integrating young adult literature into all subjects we encourage a broader understanding of subject area content. Students can learn about historical and scientific processes through the exploration of biographies of individuals who were instrumental in moving the thinking of those disciplines forward.

Students can learn about the sociological forces that influenced the thinking of individuals who made great intellectual and practical breakthroughs. Students will be encouraged to read a variety of genres and understand how each genre is effective for delivering different types of messages.

Second, decisions and commitment to giving teachers latitude in developing and in using strategies and assessment appropriate for the students that they teach is important. The hope is through the use and suggestions of a "Learning Communities" model for professional development a broadened view of teaching literature, specifically young adult literature, is implemented.

Selecting Appropriate Young Adult Books

Third, criteria related to the selection of appropriate books for young adults need to be identified so that informed decisions can be made by teachers, librarians, and parents as they choose books for young adult readers. Books such as this one can provide guidance in developing appropriate criteria for the selection of books and insight into implementing strategies that maximize the potential for student learning and personal growth.

Role of Libraries and Resource Centers

Finally, libraries and resource centers should be established and organized to support the changes in structure, purpose, and organization to support the decisions that are made with regard to what we have said about these upper-level decisions and guidelines for implementation.

All stakeholders need to be included in these decision-making processes for the implications of what we have presented throughout this book to be implemented and be successful in the instruction and assessment of young adults' abilities to read literature.

SUMMING UP

Chapter 6 attempts to synthesize and apply the ideas from chapters 1 through 5 to illustrate the implications for curriculum and implementation of those ideas. The goal is to bring some useful understandings about everything that we have said throughout the book to those individuals and groups who are responsible for planning and implementing these ideas in schools, specifically with regards to the use of young adult literature. The hope is that this summation in chapter 6 makes these ideas concrete enough to guide decision-makers and stakeholders in their implementation of the ideas in schooling.

Background Reading and Bibliographic References

Abrams, M.H. (1953). *The Mirror and the Lamp.* New York: Oxford University Press.

Alvermann, D.E. (2001). *Effective Literacy Instruction for adolescents.* Chicago, IL: National Reading Conference.

Anderson, L.W. and Krathwohl, D.R. (2001). *A Taxonomy for Teaching, Learning, and Assessing: A Revision of Bloom's Taxonomy of Educational Objectives.* New York: Longman.

Anderson, M. and Jiang, J. (2018). *Teens, Social Media & Technology.* Pew Research Center.

Applebee, A.N. (1974). *Tradition and Reform in the Teaching of English.* Urbana, IL: NCTE.

Anderson, P. (2007). What is Web 2.0? Ideas, technologies and implications for education. *JISC Technology and Standards Watch*, 2–64.

Armstrong, T. (2000). *Multiple Intelligences in the Classroom.* Washington DC: Association of School Curriculum Development.

Banister, S. (2008). Web 2.0 tools in the reading classroom: Teachers exploring literacy in the 21st century. *International Journal of Technology in Teaching and Learning*, 4(2), 109–116.

Barricelli, J-P. and Gibaldi, J. (eds.). (1980). *Interrelations of Literature.* New York: The Modern Language Association of America.

Barth, R. (1975). *The Pleasure of the Text.* New York: Hill & Want.

Bateman, C.B. and Murrie, D.C. (2003). *Adolescent Peer Culture.* Washington, D.C.: Encyclopedia of Education.

Beach, R. and Marshall, J. (1990). *Teaching Literature in the Secondary School.* Belmont, CA: Wadsworth/Thomson Learning.

Bean, T.W. and Dunkerly-Bean, J. (2014). *Teaching Young Adult Literature: Developing Students as World Citizens.* Thousand Oaks, CA: Sage Publications, Inc.

Benton, M. and Fox, G. (1985). *Teaching Literature.* London: Oxford University Press.

Benton, M, Teasy, J., Bell, R. and York, K. (1988). *Young Readers Responding to Poems.* New York: Routledge.

Bloom, B.S. (1956). *Taxonomy of Educational Objectives: The Classification of Educational Goals.* New York: Longmans, Green.

Boeree, C.G. (2006). Erikson, E. Retrieved from: http://webspace.ship.edu/cgboer/erikson.html.

Bronfenbrenner, U. (1912). Ecological systems theories. In R. Vasta (ed.), *Six Theories of Child Development – Revised Formations* (pp. 184–249). Jessical Kingsley Publishers: APA Psych.Net.

Bronfenbrenner, U. (2000). in Kazdin, A.E. (ed.), *Encyclopedia of Psychology*, Vol. 3 (pp. 121–133). Washington, D.C. APA New York: Oxford Press.

Brooks, D. (2015). *The road to character.* New York: Random House.

Brown, B.B. (1989). The role of peer groups in adolescents' adjustment to secondary school. In T. Berndt G. Ladd, G. (eds.), *Peer Relationships in Child Development.* New York: John Wiley Inc.

Campbell, J. (1988). *The Power of Myth.* New York: Doubleday.

Cart, M. (2007). Teens and the future of reading. *American Libraries,* 38(9), 52–54. JSTOR, www.jstor.org/stable/27771338.

Coiro, J. (2003). Reading comprehension on the Internet: Expanding our understanding of reading comprehension to encompass new literacies. *The Reading Teacher,* 56, 458–464.

Coiro, J., Knobel, M., Lankshear, C. and Leu, D.J. (2008). Central issues in new literacies and new literacies research. In J. Coiro, M. Knobel, C. Lankshear, & D. J. Leu (eds.), *Handbook of research on New Literacies* (pp. 1–21). New York: Lawrence Erlbaum Associates, Taylor & Francis Group.

Cooper, Charles. (1985). *Researching Response to Literature and the Teaching of Literature.* Norwood, NJ.: Ablex.

Cornell and Murie, D.C. (2012). "Adolescent peer culture". *Encyclopedia.com.* The Gale Group Inc.

Dagostino, L. and Carifio, J. (1994). *Evaluating Reading: A Cognitive View of Literacy.* Boston, MA: Allyn and Bacon, Inc.

Daniels, H. (2002). *Literature circles: Voice and choice in Student-Centered Classroom* (2nd edition). York, ME: Stenhouse.

Dewey, J. (1934/1980). *Art as Experience.* New York: Perigee Books.

Dias, P. and Hayhow, M. (1988). *Developing Response to Poetry.* London, UK: Open University Press.

Eagleton, T. (1983). *Literary Theory.* Minneapolis, MN: University of Minnesota.

Eco, U. (1979). *The Role of the Reader.* Bloomington: Indiana University Press.

Edel, L. (1955). *The Psychological Novel.* New York: Lippincott.

Edwards, P.A. (2010). Reconceptualizing literacy. *Reading Today,* 27(6), 22.

Erikson, E. (1968). *Identity: Young and Crisis.* New York: Norton Press.

Freund, Elizabeth (1987). *The Return of the Reader: Reader-response Criticism.* London, UK: Methuen.

Gardner, H. (1983). *Frames of Mind: Theory of Multiple Intelligences.* New York: Basic Books.

Gardner, H. (1999). *Intelligence reframed: Multiple intelligences for the 21st century.* New York: Basic Books.

Gardner, J. (1984). *The Art of Fiction.* New York: Knopf.

Goodman, P. (1968). *The Structure of Literature.* Chicago, IL: University of Chicago Press.

Gould, E., DiYanni, R. and Smith, W. (1987). *The Art of Reading.* New York: Random House.

Hall, G.S. (2006). In Arnett, J.S., Adolescence and Brilliance by G. Stanley Hall in *History of Psychology,* 9(3), 186–197.

Haroutunian-Gordon, S. (2009). *Learning to Teach Through Discussion: The art of turning the soul.* New Haven: Yale University Press.

Havighurst, R.J. (1956). Research on the developmental tasks concept. *The School Review,* 64(5), 213–233.

Hillocks, G. (1980). Towards a hierarchy of skills in the comprehension of literature. *English Journal,* 69, 54–59.

Hillocks, G. (1982). *The English Curriculum under Fire.* Urbana, IL: NCTE

Hirsch, E.D. (1967). *Validity in Interpretation.* New Haven: Yale University Press.

Hirsch, E.D. (1976). *Aims of Interpretation.* Chicago, IL: University of Chicago Press.

Iser, W. (1978). *The Act of Reading.* Baltimore, MD: Johns Hopkins University Press.

Kaplan, J.S. and Hayn, J. (2012). *Teaching Young Adult Literature Today: Insights, considerations, and perspectives for the Classroom Teacher.* Lanham, MD: Rowman & Littlefield.

Kappeler, S. and Norman B. (1983). *Teaching the Text.* London: Routledge.

Keene, E.O. and Zimmermann, S. (1997). *Mosaic of thought: Teaching comprehension in a Reader's Workshop.* Portsmouth, NH: Heinemann.

Larsen, B. (2018). Speaking of Psychology: The good and bad of Peer Pressure. Retrieved from The American Psychological Association website: https://www.apa.org/research/action/speaking-of-psychology/peer-pressure.

Larson, L.C. (2009). e-Reading and e-Responding: New tools for the next generation of readers. *Journal of Adolescent and Adult Literacy*, 53(3), 255–258.

Lashbrook, J.T. (2000). Fitting in: Exploring the emotional dimension of adolescent peer pressure. *Adolescence*, 35(140), 747–757.

Leavis, Q.D. (1932). *Fiction and the Reading Public.* London: Chatto and Windus.

Leitch, T. (1986). *Narrative Theory and Interpretation.* University Park, PA: Pennsylvania State University Press.

Lenhart, A., Arafeh, S., Smith, A. and Macgill, A. (2008, April 24). Writing, technology and teens. Retrieved from Pew Internet & American Life Project website: http://pewinternet.org/Reports/2008/Writing-Technology-and-Teens.aspx

Leu, Jr., D.J., Kinzer, C.K., Coiro, J. and Cammack, D.W. (2004). Toward a theory of new literacies emerging from the Internet and other information and communication technologies. In R.B. Ruddell, & N.J. Unrau (eds.), *Theoretical Models and Processes of Reading* (pp. 1570–1613). Newark, DE: International Reading Association.

Marcia, J. (1980). Identity in adolescence. In J. Adelson (ed.), *Handbook of Adolescent Psychology* (pp. 159–183). New York: Wiley.

McLeod, S.A. (2018, May 03). Erik Eriksen's Stages of Psychological Development. Retrieved from: https://www.simplypsychology.org/Erik-Erikson.html.

Miller, B.E. (1980). *Teaching the Art of Literature.* Champaign, IL: National Council of Teachers of English.

Minot, S. (1985). *Reading Fiction.* Englewood Cliffs, NJ: Prentice-Hall.

Muuss, R.E. (1965). *Theories of Adolescence.* New York: Random House.

National Council of Teachers of English Executive Committee. (2008, August 18). Position statement on Multimodal Literacies. Retrieved from: http://www.ncte.org/positions/statements/multimodalliteracies

National Endowment for the Arts. (2007). Reading at Risk: A Survey of Literary Reading in America. Research Division Report 46. Washington, D.C.: Library of Congress.

National Endowment for the Arts. (2007). To read or not to read: A question of National Consequence. Research Division Report 47. Washington, D.C..: Library of Congress.

National Endowment for the Arts. (2017). The 2017 Survey of Public Participation in the Arts. Washington, D.C.: Library of Congress.

Nicolon, R. (2000). Erikson's Psychological Stages of development. Retrieved from: http://www.psychpage.com/learning/library/person/erikson.html.

Nilsen, A.P. and Donelson, K. (2008). *Literature for Today's Young Adults.* Glenview, IL: Scott, Foresman.

Nixon, R.E. (1962). *The Art of Growing.* New York: Random House.

Odell, L. and Cooper, C. (1982). Describing responses to works of fiction. *Research in the Teaching of English*, 10, 19–36.

Overstreet, H.A. (1984). *The Mature Mind*. New York: W. W. Norton & Company.

Owen, M. (2003). Developing a love of literature: Why young adult literature is important. *Orana,* 39(1), 11–16.

Paquette, D. and Ryan, J. (2001, July 21). Bronfenbrenner's Ecological System Theory. Retrieved from: http://www.cms-kids.com/providers/early_steps/training/documents/bronfenbrenners_ecological.pdf.

Perl, S. and Wilson, S. (1986). *Through Teachers' Eyes*. Portsmouth, NH: Heinemann.

Pew Research Center. (June 12, 2019). Social Media Fact Sheet. Retrieved from Pew Internet & Technology website: https://www.pewresearch.org/internet/fact-sheet/social-media.

Position Statement on Multimodal Literacies. (2005, November). Urbana, Illinois: National Council of Teachers of English. Retrieved from National Council of Teachers of English website: http://www.ncte.org/positions/statements/multimodalliteracies.

Probst, R. (1985). *Adolescent Literature: Response and Analysis.* Columbus, OH: Charles Merrill.

Protherough, R. (1986). *Developing Response to Fiction.* Philadelphia: Open University Press.

Purves, A. (1981). *Reading and Literature*. Urbana, IL: NCTE.

Retzinger, S.M. (1995). Identifying shame and anger in discourse. *American Behavioral Scientist* 38, 114–1113.

Richard, I.A. (1929). *Practical Criticism*. New York: Harcourt Brace.

Rockas, L. (1984). *Ways in: Analyzing and Responding to Literature.* Portsmouth, NH: Boynton-Cook.

Rosenblatt, Louise. (1978). *The Reader, The Text, The Poem.* Carbondale: Southern Illinois University Press.

Rosenblatt, L.M. (1995). *Literature as Exploration* (5th edition). New York: Modern Language Association.

Rosenblatt, L.M. (2005). *Making Meaning with Texts: Selected Essays.* Portsmouth, NH: Heinemann Press.

Rudolph, K. (2010). Implicit theories of peer relationships. *Social Development,* 19(1), 113–119.

Said, Edward (1984). *The World, the Text and the Critic.* London: Faber and Faber.

Santosa, M.H. (2008, June). Podcasting in English classroom? Why Not?. Paper presented at Seminar Nasional Aplikasi Teknologi, Yogyakarta, Indonesia.

Sarte, J.-P. (1978). *What is Literature?* London: Peter Smith.

Scholes, R. (1985). *Textual Power: Literary Theory and the Teaching of English.* New Haven: Yale University Press.

Smith, F. (1982). *Writing and the writer.* London: Heinemann Educational Books.

Smith, N.B. (2002). *American Reading Instruction.* Newark, DE: International Reading Association.

Smolin, L.I. and Lawless, K.A. (2003). Becoming literate in the technological age: New responsibilities and tools for teachers. *The Reading Teacher,* 56(6), 570–577.

Squire, J. (1985). Studying response to literature through school surveys. In Charles Cooper (ed.), *Researching Response to Literature and the Teaching of Literature.* Norwood, NJ: Ablex.

Sternberg, R.J. (1985). Implicit theories of intelligence, creativity and wisdom. *Journal of Personality and Social Psychology,* 49(3), 607–627.

Sumara, Dennis, J. (2002). *Why Reading Literature in School Still Matters: Imagination, Interpretation, Insight.* Mahwah, NJ: Lawrence J. Erlbaum Publishers.

Svensson, C. (1985) *The Construction of Poetic Meaning.* Uppsals, Sweden: Liber.

Tompkins, J. (1980). *Reader-response Criticism.* Baltimore, MD: John Hopkins University Press.

Tracey, D. and Morrow, L. (2017). *Lenses on reading: An introduction to theories and models.* New York: The Guilford Press.

Twinge, J.M., Martin, G.N. and Spitzberg, B.H. (2019). Trends in U.S. adolescents' media use, 1976-2016: The rise of digital media, the decline of TB, and the (near) demise of print. *Psychology of Popular Media Culture,* 8(4), 329–345.

Wellek, R. and Warren, A. (1956). *The Theory of Literature.* New York: Harcourt Brace and Company.

West, K.C. (2008). Weblogs and literary response: Socially situated identities and hybrid social languages in English class blogs. *Journal of Adolescent and Adult Literacy,* 51(7), 588–599.

Williams, Raymond. (1958). *Culture and Society.* London: Penguin.

Williams, D. (December 2007/January 2008). Changing classroom practice. *Educational Leadership,* 65(4) 36–42.

TRADE BOOKS INCLUDED IN THE TEXT

Anderson, L.H. (1999). *Speak.* New York: Farrar Straus Giroux.
Austen, J. (1992). *Emma,* 6th ed. New York: St. Martin's Press.
Chbosky, S. (1999). *The Perks of Being a Wallflower.* New York: Pocket Books.
Dickens, C. (2003). *Great Expectations,* 2nd ed. London: Penguin Classics.
Green, J. (2017). *Turtles All the Way Down.* New York: Dutton Books.

Head, A. (1967). *Mr. and Mrs. Bo Jones.* New York: Scholastic.
Hinton, S.E. (1967). *The Outsiders.* New York: Viking Press.
Hinton, S.E. (1971). *That Was Then, This is Now.* New York: Viking Press.
Hinton, S.E. (1979): *Tex.* New York: Delacorte Press.
Hubbard, J. (2014). *And We Stay.* New York: Delacorte Press.
Kline, C.B. (2013) *Orphan Train.* New York: Harper Collins.
Knowles, J. (1959). *A Separate Peace.* London: Penguin Random House.
Lowry, L. (1993). *The Giver.* Boston, MA: Houghton-Mifflin.
Paschal, F. (1983). *Sweet Valley Twins.* New York, Random House.
Pérez, A.H. (2015). *Out of Darkness.* Minneapolis, MN: Carolrhoda Books.
Rowling, J.K. (1998). *Harry Potter and the Sorcerer's Stone.* New York: Arthur Levine Books.
Saenz, B.A. (2012). *Aristotle and Dante Discover the Secrets of the Universe.* New York: Simon and Schuster.
Salinger, J.D. (1951). *The Catcher in the Rye.* London: Penguin Books.
Satrapi, M. (2007) *The Complete Persepolis.* New York: Pantheon.
Shakespeare, W. (1985). *Romeo and Juliet,* 7th ed. Hauppage: New York: Barron's.
Smith, L.J. (1991). *The Vampire Diaries.* New York: Harper Books.
Thomas, A. (2017). *The Hate u Give.* New York: Balzer & Bray.
Twain, M. (1996). *Adventures of Huckleberry Finn,* 6th ed. New York: Random House.
Zindel, P. (1968). *The Pigman.* New York: Harper and Row.
Zindel, P. (1969). *My Darling My Hamburger.* New York: Harper and Row.

Additional Suggested YAL Books to Incorporate into the Curriculum

Acevedo, E. (2018). *The Poet X.* New York: Quill Tree Books.
Adeyemi, T. (2018). *Children of Blood and Bone.* New York: Henry Holt and Co.
Ahmadi, A. (2018). *Down and Across.* New York: Viking Books for Young Readers.
Ahmed, S. (2018). *Love, Hate, and Other Filters.* New York: Soho Teen.
Callender, K. (2020). *Felix Ever After.* New York: Balzer + Bray.
De la Cruz, M. (2016). *Something in Between.* New York: Harlequin Teen.
Flake, S.G. (2000). *The Skin I'm In.* New York: Little, Brown Books for Young Readers.
Gino, G. (2015). *George.* New York: Scholastic.
Hiranandani, V. (2018). *The Night Diary.* New York: Puffin Books.
Johnson, K. (2020). *This is My America.* New York: Random House Books for Young Readers.
Reynolds, J. and Kiely, B. (2017). *All American Boys.* New York: Atheneum/Caitlyn Dlouhy Books.
Ribay, R. (2018). *After the Shot Drops.* New York: HMH Books for Young Readers.

Rivera, G. (2016). *Juliet Takes a Breath*. New York: Riverdale Avenue Books.

Rivera, L. (2017). *The Education of Margot Sanchez*. New York: Simon & Schuster Books for Young Readers.

Saedi, S. (2018). *Americanized: Rebel Without a Green* Card. New York: Ember.

Sánchez, E.L. (2017). *I Am Not Your Perfect Mexican Daughter*. New York: Alfred. A. Knop.

Senzai, N.H. (2018). *Escape from Aleppo*. New York: Simon & Schuster /Paula Wiseman Books.

Stone, N. (2017). *Dear Martin*. New York: Crown Books for Young Readers.

Sugiura, M. (2017). *It's Not Like It's a Secret*. New York: Harper Teen.

Woodson, J. (2016). *Brown Girl Dreaming*. New York: Puffin Books.

Yang, G.L. (2006). *American Born Chinese*. New York: First Second.

Zobi, I. (2017). *American Street*. New York: Balzer + Bray.

About the Authors

Dr. Lorraine Dagostino, professor emeritus, University of Massachusetts Lowell, has been an educator since 1970 in the public schools, community college, four-year college, and the university. She received her degrees from Russell Sage College, the College of St. Rose, and Syracuse University. Her teaching in the public school was in history, English, and reading. In the community college, she taught study skills class for preparation for college. At the college and university, her work has been in many aspects of reading instruction and theory along with literacy research studies with graduate students at the master's and doctoral level of study. She has published numerous journal articles and books in these areas of study, and was awarded best paper awards from NERA, EERA, and distinguished papers from AERA. She has presented professional papers at State, Regional, National, and International Conferences. She has been president of the New England Philosophy of Education Society and the Massachusetts Association of Reading Educators. She also did work at Harvard University as a research associate. Her personal interests are traveling and swimming along with volunteer work for various organizations. She is a Paul Harris Fellow from Rotary International.

Dr. Kathleen Ryan received a BA from Boston College in English, an MA from the University College Dublin, Ireland, in Anglo-Irish Literature, MEd from Boston College in Language and Literacy, and an EdD in Language Arts and Literacy from University of Massachusetts Lowell. She is an associate professor at Hellenic College in Brookline, Massachusetts. Dr. Ryan is the codirector of the Literature and History Department and also the director of the Education Program which offers a Minor in Education. Dr. Ryan joined the Hellenic College faculty in 2004 with a wide range of experience in the fields of Literature and Literacy. Her past work experiences include the positions of literacy specialist and literacy coach in the public schools as well as with young adults in public housing developments. Her research focuses on the power of literature to transform both academic lives and personal lives. Her presentations and publications focus on the importance of nurturing personal responses to literature. Her research reflects her belief in the power of literature and its capacity to serve as an agent of empathy, insight, and compassion. Throughout her career, her research and teaching has been shaped by a belief in the transformative power of teaching, learning, and literature.

Dr. Jennifer Bauer is the chair of the Communication Department at Middlesex Community College. Prior to that, she taught at Lowell High School for twelve years, as well as summer teaching positions with MS2 at Phillips Academy Andover, and Urban Scholars at the University of Massachusetts, Boston. She also spent fifteen years coaching crew at the middle school, high school, collegiate, and master's levels. Dr. Bauer is an award-winning blogger and filmmaker and has had her writing published online at the Huffington Post, Outdoor Families Magazine, theBump, and the National Park Foundation. She earned her BS in Video Production from Ithaca College, her MFA in Film Production from Boston University, her MEd in Curriculum & Instruction from Pennsylvania State University, and her PhD in Literacy Studies from the University of Massachusetts Lowell. Her published work and conferences papers focus on the educational inequities faced by English Language Learners in the classroom, as well as language variation and code switching. In her free time, she spends a lot of time hiking and camping with her wife and kids, and way too much time watching television and movies.

www.ingramcontent.com/pod-product-compliance
Lightning Source LLC
Chambersburg PA
CBHW052049300426
44117CB00012B/2050